Bristol Short Story Prize Anthology

Volume Twelve

tangent books

Bristol Short Story Prize Anthology Volume 12

First published 2019 by Tangent Books

Tangent Books
Unit 5.16 Paintworks
Bristol
BS4 3EH
0117 972 0645
www.tangentbooks.co.uk

Email: richard@tangentbooks.co.uk

ISBN: 9781910089880

Cover designed by Naomi Clarke

Layout designed by Dave Oakley, Arnos Design
www.arnosdesign.co.uk

Printed and bound by ScandinavianBook.co.uk
c/o LaserTryk.co.uk Ltd.
Hamilton House, Mabledon Place
Bloomsbury, WC1H 9BB

A CIP catalogue record for this book is available from the British Library
www.tangentbooks.co.uk
www.bristolprize.co.uk

Contents

Introduction

Welcome to the 12th edition of the Bristol Short Story Prize! I could not be prouder of the 20 stories that have made it into these pages. These stories – and the 20 more that made it onto the longlist – stood out from 2,495 strong entries, which we received from writers based in 80 different countries.

The writers' own settings made for an incredible variety of voices, and though there were common themes running through many of them (it seems things feel a little dark right now no matter where you are...), it was deeply rewarding to spend a few thousand words looking at our world through someone else's eyes. As borders are being built around us, storytelling is still one of our best tools for breaking those walls back down again – to build empathy, to show us other ways of living, to help us resist a too narrow vision of ourselves and our place on this planet.

Our top three stories from Cameron Stewart, Cherise Saywell, and S. Bhattacharya-Woodward took us from Tasmania to the Rockefeller Center to Moscow and to an unnamed council estate and the inner world of a boy whose imagination lets him escape its bricks and concrete. And the 17 stories that follow also send us exploring other lands, languages, and lives.

Reading is always a subjective experience, especially so with the breadth and range we received, and my fellow judges Lucy Cowie, Polly Ho-Yen, Billy Kahora and I found something remarkable in every story we read. The debate was lively, and each story touched us in both unique and universal ways. It is a brave act to send your writing into the world, and we are grateful for the opportunity to consider them. Thank you.

And thanks to University of the West of England Illustration degree course leaders, Chris Hill and Jonathan Ward, who run the annual anthology cover design project with their final year students from which this beautiful cover by Naomi Clarke was selected.

And now: I hope you'll love the following pages as much as I do, that you'll meet new worlds and characters along the way, and perhaps even recognize yourself in them. Enjoy the journey.

Kate Johnson

1ˢᵗ Prize

Cameron Stewart

Cameron Stewart lives in Sydney, Australia. He grew up on a farm near Mullumbimby, by way of Alice Springs, Canberra and Cairns. Diversity of place informs much of his writing, as does an interest in flawed characters trying to do their best. Cameron has short fiction in *Subtropics, The London Magazine* and the *2019 UTS Writers' Anthology - Infinite Threads*. A graduate of Western Sydney University (BA Performing Arts), Cameron is currently studying an MA in Creative Writing, at the University of Technology, Sydney. He is also currently working on his first collection of short stories.

Black Snow

A few miles out of town on a dirt road in bushland, my father pulled over and parked in a shallow ditch. 'Stay in the car,' he threw at me over his shoulder. Doors opened and closed, and he and Leah walked off with a blanket and a clinking bag of bottles. Leah was my father's girlfriend. She looked after me when he worked in the mines, but now he was home for good. I locked the doors and pulled out a book my uncle gave me for my birthday. It was about a man and a boy walking around in the cold trying to avoid people who wanted to eat them. What kind of present is that? I prefer to read something real, like science. Threads of sunlight filtered through shifting trees and angled into the cabin. A logging truck rumbled by, pluming dust. Hours passed. It was autumn in Tasmania, and the sun dropped like a shot duck. There was an old towel in the back which I threw over my shoulders for warmth. My toes felt like pebbles in cold river water. Tracing patterns on the leather seats, I picked at some broken stitching. In the glovebox, I found papers, chewed pens, lipstick, a few coins – and a butter knife.

'Why did you do it?' my father yelled at me later. 'Why the fuck did you do it? Is there something wrong with your head?'

I asked him if there was something wrong with his head.

'Watch your mouth,' he said, 'or I'll knock your block off.'

Leah told him to take it easy.

'Should make the little cunt walk,' said my father.

I wished he'd just hit me and be done with it. If pressed, I'd say that the popping sound the butter knife made as I punched it through the leather made me feel good. I knew what I was doing was wrong and at first thought I'd only stab one hole, a hole that wouldn't be noticed, but once I got started I couldn't stop.

South of the tropical city of Cairns, a violent updraft rushed five thousand feet up the steep ridge of the mountain. Rainforest and a summit strewn with granite boulders stood shrouded in mist and rain. As the plane shuddered through a column of swirling, black cloud, and yawed east towards the sea, I wondered why I was being sent to stay with my uncle at the other end of the country. Water droplets shimmered and flicked across my window like shattered beads of mercury. The fuselage vibrated in buffeting wind and a lone, green light blinked on the wingtip. There was no hand to hold. Suddenly the aircraft dropped into blinding light. Into sunshine. Into safety. I surveyed paddocks of wet sugar cane that gridded the earth.

The first thing that struck me, stepping off the plane, was the tropical air. Beyond the heat and jet fuel were smells hard to identify, smells I'd soon be steeped in – damp earth and molasses, mangoes and diesel, papayas, compost and custard apples, burnt sugar and stale beer. Burning cane. Approaching thunderstorms. Ash.

Uncle John was waiting in the arrivals lounge – legs smeared in mud. Shoeless. A scar ran from cheekbone to lip making him look mean.

'You caught me in the middle of something,' he said as we walked to his dented Landrover. Heat rose off the bitumen carpark.

'Might want to lose the jacket and the jeans,' he added. 'And the shoes.'

Half an hour later we wadded barefoot across the mudflats of the Cairns esplanade, shin deep in stinking mud. I struggled to keep up. The tide was low, and we headed out a fair way. Uncle John pointed out birds I'd never heard of – spoonbills, plovers, knots and curlews.

'See that little one?' he said, pointing to a group of seabirds feeding on the mud. He handed me his binoculars. I recognised a pelican.

'To the left of that,' he said. 'Tiny one with black legs and a black bill. Mottled on top. White underneath.'

'Yeah, I see it.'

'It's a red-necked stint.'

Don't know what he expected me to say. The bird looked nondescript. Drab.

'Weighs less than a box of matches,' said my uncle. 'Flew over ten thousand kilometres from Siberia to get here. It'll fly further than from here to the moon in its lifetime.'

I wondered how long I'd have to stay here.

My uncle lives on the city outskirts in a two bedroom weatherboard that backs onto a mountain range. At the bottom of the hill over the railway tracks is a creek, and stretched out beyond that are cane fields. Uncle John tells me that during the last cyclone, they all went under water.

I sleep on a mattress in an enclosed veranda. There's no cupboard – I live out of my suitcase. At night I lie naked under an overhead fan that goes full tilt, testing the screws that anchor it to the ceiling. I can see the moon through the window – each night it gets a little smaller as it wanes. Outside, a large mango tree drops its fruit on the ground. Bush turkeys and rats rip them to pieces. I hear scratching and gnawing at night and see torn pulp in the grass the next day. The iron roof creaks and clunks as the day heats up, and most afternoons there's a thunderstorm which steams off the hot roads. It never gets cold.

The second bedroom is used as a study. Uncle John's desk sits under the window, surrounded by books. Makeshift shelves of planks on bricks carry volumes on birds, insects, bats, butterflies, reptiles, mammals – anything zoological. Stacks of journals sit on the wooden floor and a bar fridge full of beer hums under the desk. Uncle John leaves for work before I get up. It's school holidays so I do my own thing.

After a couple of weeks I call home but no-one picks up. I figure my old man and Leah must've gone on holiday. Somewhere remote. Once, Dad took me camping for my birthday. My teacher said I'd be able to see Jupiter and Venus if the night sky was clear but I couldn't find them, and Dad wasn't interested. He wanted to take me duck shooting instead but I didn't want to. 'What's wrong with you?' he said. We ate cheese sandwiches that Leah had made. It was nice to sit with him around the fire.

'Hey Fuckface! Check this out.' Hank beckons me over. On a small hill overlooking the creek sits a caravan with flat tires. Hank lays his bike down and creeps forward. He picks up a rock.

Hank lives a few streets over. I met him last week at the shops and he's been showing me around. He's a bit older than me.

Yesterday, we had a mango fight with some kids in Cassowary Street. Then we jumped the back fence of a big house up the hill. No-one was home so we swam in the pool. There was a little black and white terrier in the yard – a 'Ratdog,' my Dad would've called it. Hank chucked him into the pool and kept throwing him back in the middle whenever he paddled to the edge. This was pretty funny for a while, but it got to the stage where I didn't know if Hank was going to stop, so I pulled a couple of my uncle's beer cans out of my bag to distract him. When the dog finally dragged himself out, he went over to Hank for a pat. We drank a can each, and offered some to the dog, but it wasn't interested. I pretended to enjoy dangling my feet in the water but I was scared the owners would turn up.

'You don't talk much, do ya?' said Hank.

I couldn't think what to say back to him.

'How long you here?' he asked.

'Dunno,' I said. 'Maybe another week. School starts soon.'

'Ever seen snow?'

'Yeah,' I said, 'I'm from Tassie.'

'Tomorrow I wanna show you something,' he said.

Then he pissed into the pool. I pulled my feet out.

Last night Uncle John cooked a curry. He got me to cut up some beef into chunks. Then he fried them in a pan with onions and spices and simmered it in vegetable stock and tomatoes. He taught me how to wash the rice before steaming it.

'Takes the starch out,' he said.

Dropping papadums into hot oil and watching them slowly curl was my favourite bit. My uncle showed me how to press down gently with a spatula to keep them flat. I fried up a stack.

'Give me a hand after dinner eh?' he asked from across the kitchen.

'Okay,' I replied.

'I wanna move all my books into the veranda,' he said.

I stopped fishing out cutlery. Uncle John had his back to me, spooning curry into bowls.

'Where will I sleep?' I asked.

'In the study,' said my uncle. 'We'll make it your bedroom.'

Over dinner, Uncle John alternated his attention between curry and beer while I crunched my way through some papadums. There were things I wanted to ask him, but I wasn't sure how and I was scared of the answers.

'Where's Dad?' I said.

My uncle sat back in his chair and wiped his hands up and down on his shorts. Then he lifted his head and looked right at me. His scar stood out against his tanned face but he didn't look mean.

'Back in the mines,' he said.

The words hung in the air for a while and I tried to unpick them.

'But he's stopped doing that,' I said. 'He's back home now. For good.'

My uncle didn't say anything.

'What about Leah?' I asked. 'Where's she?'

'I don't know mate.'

Late afternoon the next day I cycled down to Hanks. His two brothers were doing backflips off the veranda and his Mum was mowing the backyard. I found Hank in the garage searching through a pile of junk. He pulled out an old cricket bat and tied it onto his bike rack.

'Do you like music?' he asked.

'Sure.'

'What do you listen to?'

Nothing came to mind. We didn't play much music at home.

'I don't know,' I said. 'Whatever sounds good.'

Although the sun was dipping, the heat was still strong. I stepped over clumps of prickles as we wheeled our bikes across the lawn. Hank walked right over them. After three weeks, my feet had toughened up, but nothing compared to Hank. His feet were pure callus. He reckoned he could put a cigarette out on them.

We cycled down the hill and stopped at the edge of Kamerunga Road. Trucks and four-wheel-drives barrelled past on the cracked bitumen. The air smelled of molasses from the sugar mill, and mountains loomed in the distance. When there was a break in the traffic, we crossed, bumping our way over the train tracks and freewheeling across the causeway. We pedalled up a narrow track that ran between the creek and paddocks of sugar cane.

'Ever had a fuck?' Hank asked out of the blue.

I replied honestly. After all I was only thirteen.

'Me neither,' said Hank. We kept pedalling.

'Ever seen anyone doing it?' he added.

'Nup.' I didn't want to talk about stuff like that.

Hank threw a rock at the caravan perched on the hill. It pinged off the front door. Nothing moved.

'Captain Jack lives there', said Hank. 'Old navy bloke with a wooden leg.'

'A wooden leg?'

'Yeah, like a pirate. No bullshit. I reckon he's been in jail. He used to have a cockatoo. Taught it how to say "not guilty." My brother reckons he's a kiddy fiddler.'

I couldn't think of what to say.

Hank laughed. 'Don't worry,' he said. 'No-one's home. His car's not here.'

'How does he drive with one leg?'

'Must use an automatic, eh?' said Hank. 'Pussy.'

We rode down a dirt track between fields of cane the height of two men. The air was tacky and my t-shirt stuck to my back. I wondered why we were pedalling away from the creek and not towards it – why everything went opposite to how I wanted.

Hank hopped off his bike and untied the cricket bat. He hit it against a cane stalk until it split, then levered out a piece of fibre from inside. I followed Hank's lead and chewed it for a bit – sucked out the juice and spat out the woody pulp. Tasted a bit like vanilla. Then Hank pulled out a cigarette lighter and crouched down. He laid the tiny flame against some leaf litter at the base of the sugar cane. Black smoke drifted in thin fingers.

'This is what I wanted to show you,' he said.

We kept cycling but Hank stopped regularly to light more fires. Over my shoulder I could see plumes of black smoke drifting over the cane and heard the light crackle of fire catching.

When we reached the end of the track, Hank hooked right and kept pedalling. I struggled to keep up. Once we got at the opposite side of the paddock from where the first fire was lit, he hopped off his bike. We shared a drink of water and waited.

Hank told me that his great grandfather was kidnapped from the Solomon Islands to work in the cane fields and how his grandad and old man worked their whole lives there too. He told me that back in the day they'd have a big burn-off before the harvest – how snakes and rats, scorpions, wasps and bandicoots all lived in the cane, and that during the burn-off, the hawks and eagles circled, looking for an easy feed when the animals tried to escape.

By now the sun had dropped and a breeze had kicked up. Black smoke swept over the field, and flakes of ash and cinders swirled high in the twilight. The fire howled as it intensified and flames shot ten metres out of the cane tops and thickened into a block of fire.

Hank stood ready with the cricket bat in his hand, his forehead shone, and overhead, a couple of hawks hovered. A rat shot past. Then another. Up the track I saw a snake slide into the next paddock. Then a bandicoot hopped out of the cane and stopped in front of us. The smell of burning fur and burnt sugar hit my nostrils. Hank stepped forward and clubbed the animal over the head. I turned away and started coughing from the smoke and heard the bandicoot get hit again.

'Why did you do that?' I yelled, over the roar of the fire.

'Put it out of its misery!' he yelled back at me.

Another bandicoot scuttled out and Hank cracked it across the skull. Then he picked it up by the tail and lobbed it into the blaze – turned to me with a big smile on his face.

The smoke increased as the wind gusted and I shielded my face from the heat. Another bandicoot hobbled out of the fire. One side of it was burnt raw and there was something wrong with its back leg. The animal paused on the track between the two paddocks – one green, one ablaze. Hank handed me the bat. I looked at the mountains and wished I was somewhere else. Hank grabbed the bandicoot by the tail but it didn't struggle so he let go and stepped backwards. I didn't want to hit him more than once so I lifted the bat high.

My old man wouldn't think I had it in me. I tried to think of when father's face didn't have a disappointed expression. I remembered a few years back when some miners were trapped underground in Chile. I couldn't sleep at night, and he'd scoffed.

'Don't worry about me,' he said. 'I just drive the trucks.'

But I wasn't worried about him – I knew he drove trucks. I wasn't stupid. I worried for the men in the dark. The men underground –

whether they'd be buried alive.

I swung the bat down hard. Far away, Hank was yelling but I kept hitting the little animal. Then an ember scorched the top of my hand and I stopped. Plumes of sparks poured into the sky and the bandicoot lay in a lumpy mess at my feet. My eyes started to water. They streamed. The fire had leapt to the green paddock and began to flare-up. Hank was jumping up and down, yelling and waving at the end of the track – a shimmering figure through heat and smoke. I watched hairs on my arms pucker and shrivel and heard booming thunder and sirens in the distance.

We zig-zagged through spot fires, raining ash and falling embers, back towards the creek. Bikes abandoned, our feet flopped in warm black ash.

'Snow!' yelled Hank. 'Black snow!'

Rain fell on my face. Pouring rain.

When Uncle John woke me later that night it was pitch black and the rain had stopped. The world was quiet. I was in my new bedroom. I don't know what the time was.

'Get dressed and get in the car,' said my uncle. He handed me the jacket and jeans I'd worn when I first arrived.

We drove for about an hour. Out of town and into the mountains. The moon had vanished and it was difficult to make out if the sky was overcast, or totally clear. As the Landrover swept around each hairpin, the headlights briefly illuminated thick forest. Sometimes I glimpsed the coast out my window – far, far below. A dim gleam on dark water. The city lights twinkled lightly on the fringe before fading into nothing, and the top of my hand throbbed where it had been burned. A bandage of gauze and surgical tape covered the injury. Uncle

John must have dressed the wound last night, but I don't remember this happening. I tried to remember my father's face, but was having difficulty. Uncle John kept driving onwards and upwards, corner after corner. I nodded off.

When I was shaken awake, the car had stopped, and the engine was off. I felt cold. First time I'd been cold since Tasmania. Reaching out, I touched the chill of the windscreen. I couldn't see my uncle in the darkness, but I heard him beside me.

'Here,' he said, guiding my fingers around a container. 'Watch yourself. It's a thermos.'

I had a sip. Hot chocolate. I thanked him.

Uncle John got out and closed his door. He crunched around the bonnet, to my side. He helped me get out.

'Hold my hand,' he said. I gave him my good one.

My feet pressed into mud and twigs as he led me up a track. Sometimes he paused to push aside a branch or help me over a log. The forest thrummed with the drone of insects and frogs, the dripping of water, the flapping of wings. Sporadic crashes sounded in the thickets – animals or fallen branches. The earth groaned with life. The blackness was crushing. I couldn't sense depth or distance and allowed myself to be pulled along.

Then my uncle slowed and let go of my hand. I stepped forward and stood by his side. In the distance, floating in the night, was something from dreams. A horizontal plane of pulsing light. Luminescence. Blues and greens, yellows and whites – like jewels. We stepped closer. My uncle's face looked like a child's – like how I felt. In wonder. He put his arm around me and drew me in close. He gripped me. We stood in front of the bank cutting, thick with glow worms. A glittering universe stretched out before us.

2ⁿᵈ Prize
Cherise Saywell

Cherise Saywell is a novelist and short-story writer. She was born and brought up in Australia and has lived in Scotland since 1996. She has published two novels, *Desert Fish* and *Twitcher*. Cherise's stories have won the Pin Drop Short Story Award, the Mslexia Short Story Prize and the V.S. Pritchett Prize. They have appeared in *Mslexia, The London Magazine* and *New Writing Scotland*, as well as in several anthologies. Her story, *Pieces of Mars Have Fallen to Earth,* was selected for BBC Radio 4's *Opening Lines* programme in 2015. She lives in Edinburgh with her family.

Fellow Travellers

On the 8th of November, 1957, a man stands on the roof of the RCA Building on Rockefeller Plaza in New York in the cold pre-dawn watching a sky bloated with black, prickled with stars. His winter coat is buttoned over a sweater. A woollen hat covers his ears. He is not alone – others have gathered here, high above the streets, and all around the city on the tallest buildings are many more watchers, waiting. Some murmur quietly, some keep silent. Soon, a tiny light tumbles into view, cutting a path along the southern horizon through the dregs of the night: Sputnik 2 – entering the sixth day of its journey. Somewhere inside that light is a slim airtight compartment containing a small stray dog. Laika. The name is one of many. Here, in New York, she is Muttnik, reported to have coped well with the violent entry into orbit. She has even eaten a space meal.

The man follows the frail light, aware of the helter-skelter of his heart – it is the world's second artificial satellite, the first to contain a living creature, moving at five miles a second out there. Binoculars in place, the man fumbles with the focus ring; his ungloved hands are cold. He would like to open up the darkness, bring the capsule closer, see in.

When the light vanishes, the man puts his binoculars away. The watchers compare notes, making sense of what they have seen by declaring what they know – that the capsule is more than 600 miles above the earth, that it completes each orbit in seventy-two minutes. The man imagines what he'll tell his young sons. His wife will bring them in when she wakes him before lunch. He might say that he saw the dog eating its dinner in space. Or that there is a window through which it can see the planets, the immense blue of the ocean below, its kennel in Kazakhstan. He will tell them it is on an adventure, that it is not afraid.

He is pleased, thinking of this, but as he fastens his bag, inexplicably he recalls a woman he once loved, and it is as if someone has knocked the air out of him. He met her during the war, when he was on leave in her home town. He remembers even now his pressing need to be with her, and how she made him less afraid of what lay ahead. He promised they would be together after the war, and in Germany, when everything felt like absence – the blasted cities, people blank and faceless – she made him feel he could return to his life whole. She wrote to him every day.

He has not thought of her for a long time.

After he was de-commissioned he asked her to join him in New York. But when she did, he was surprised to find he no longer loved her. In order to avoid the suspicion of his landlady, they had decided that the woman would not leave his apartment and during the days she was there he found it hard to speak, so he let her talk. But her voice was too loud and he wanted to put his hand over her mouth and whisper that things were different now.

The nights were easier. In the dark, the banality of sex was a welcome relief. His body was an instrument that could be relied upon to perform unrehearsed. But he couldn't bear the mornings and soon felt an urgent need to end the relationship. In order to do this swiftly, he engineered a discovery by his landlady. He made sure he was at work when this happened, and when he returned the woman had gone, he wasn't sure where.

He did not answer her letters. He did not take her calls.

Carefully now, as he takes himself out of the empty lobby and into the creeping dawn, he puts that woman out of his mind.

The man does not sleep late as planned. He rests for just an hour and rises without waking his wife, slipping past the closed door of his sons' bedroom. He is not expected at his office until afternoon, so he walks to the library. All the way there he thinks of the dog. When he rounds a corner, she seems to slope into view, head down, keeping low and almost out of sight. A stray, he knows from his time in the ruined cities of Europe, must be canny. It must keep to the edge of the frame. It will beware the hand that proffers a morsel, which might then lunge, or grasp, or snatch the food back at the last moment and put it to its own mouth, laughing. The instinct of such a creature will be to keep a safe distance from feet that might connect with the softest parts of its belly.

Laika's other names: Kudryavka, Zhuchka, Limonchik. Many dogs have been trained for these missions, but before her, none have achieved orbital flight. All are strays, selected because they will not be missed, also because they are used to cold and hunger. They tolerate being confined in tight spaces.

Laika's face is pleasant and photographs well. She has a coat with some lightness that contrasts against a dark background. Dr Yazdovsky, who prepares the dogs, describes her as quiet and charming. She bends to the will of her keepers, and succumbs to the rigours of her training, to being strapped into a harness, fitted with a waste bag. She is stoical.

Sputnik – in Russian: the one on the same path, a companion, a fellow traveller. The satellite accompanies the earth in its turning and throughout each orbit emits *bleep-bleeps*. From Ohio to Tokyo, Pretoria to Perth, radios, when tuned, pick up these sounds. Listeners strain to hear a staticky hissing, said to be the dog breathing the manufactured air. Instruments measure her heartbeat; her lungs and limbs transmit data, lines and curves that print out on graph paper in a room in Moscow, or Dnepropetrovsk, or Novosibirsk.

Several days after the sighting on Rockefeller Plaza, the transmissions cease. Laika is reported dead – euthanized or deprived of oxygen – the details are vague except to state that it was painless. The satellite continues its orbit for several months, but the man does not look for it again.

* * *

14th April, 1958. In the early hours of the morning in coastal Connecticut, a woman walks barefoot onto her front lawn. Her dressing gown flaps open over her nightie; the grass is damp and cold beneath her feet.

Inside, her husband's mother is, at last, calm. All evening she has been agitated, pacing the hall and, at bedtime, refusing to lie down. The time drags when she is erratic like this, but worse are those moments when she seems lucid. *Where did you go?* she asked at dinner, and the question seemed to come from a part of her mind still in the world. It was as if she was taking aim.

Standing now in the aftermath of her day, the woman shrugs a robed shoulder against each cheek and wipes her nose with her sleeve, wondering if, in her thirties now, she is too old to stand weeping in the night. She is no longer a girl mopping up after stupid mistakes – she has not rushed headlong into this life. She chose it.

Right then, as she looks up, in the east, there is a sudden flash, a tungsten flare that breaks and scatters – lab-bright blue, fizzing silver, white – the broken parts all moving in one direction and at such speed, shapes shifting, lengthening, shrinking.

Some kind of meteorite shower, the woman thinks. Perhaps her husband will see. He is working on a merchant vessel and will be at sea for another six weeks. The sky is different there, he has told her – it shows you everything. She likes how he confides his thoughts to her. She has loved others more fiercely, more blindly, than the way she loves her husband, but less enduringly.

She half-hopes her mother-in-law will see, that sensing something extraordinary, she might sit up and push the curtains aside. Such a spectacle might distract from the day's difficulties. It's impossible to know what stays in her head, and what fragments and dissolves. Let today dissolve, the woman thinks, the awful afternoon, the tearoom. A kind of rage came over her, and when it had passed she wondered who she'd been and if it would be possible to make amends.

She'd taken her mother-in-law to Robinson's Department Store – to buy stockings, she murmured, helping the old woman into the taxi, though what she wanted was simply to escape the house, to which she is largely confined with her husband away, when she must care for his mother alone. The thought of an outing gave her a surge of optimism; it made her delirious.

In the hosiery section the old woman touched the nylon samples, stretching the fabric over her fingers to test the colour against her skin. She waited without complaining while the purchase took place, and she remained passive, pliant, when they left the counter, pausing in her slow shuffle just once to admire the haberdashery display. Even then she was happy enough to be steered in the direction of the tearoom. It was only when they reached their table that she became restless. Unhappy with her seat, she shifted from chair to chair, increasingly discontent. Then she began to make a whimpering noise – not loud, but it disturbed the air.

The woman could easily have soothed her mother-in-law. She might have guided her gently out of the tearoom. But as she considered the best course of action, she felt a familiar clutching in her abdomen, a loosening lower down – her period, earlier than expected, so she was unprepared, but still, the drugstore was close and there was a bathroom here, right beside the service area.

But something new was in her veins. It had arrived suddenly, hot and strange, and her own true self seemed to recede to make room for it. The woman recognised this other version of herself and perhaps she welcomed it, for she saw clearly beyond each moment to what came next.

She remembers now the relief of giving in to it.

Sit down, she'd snapped, and the old woman was immediately quiet. *Now, wait here.*

At the drugstore she purchased sanitary towels, but she did not return to her mother-in-law. Instead she went to the restroom on the first floor where she took her time attending to herself. She washed her hands carefully, reapplied her lipstick before a mirror, patted her hair into place. Then she sat in a comfortable armchair in the lounge and laid her hands on her cramping belly. She put her mother-in-law quite out of her mind, but like a matter wilfully deferred rather than forgotten and when she returned to the tearoom, perhaps a half-hour later, and saw that the old woman was no longer there, she felt a kind of savage satisfaction.

Another hour passed before she happened on a salesgirl coaxing her mother-in-law out of a fitting room.

There you are. I told you to sit and wait for me, she scolded.

She turned to the girl. *I was so worried*, she said. *I was unwell, you see, and she wandered off.*

Of course, the light shower is the satellite, Sputnik 2. It has re-entered the atmosphere, disintegrating over the Caribbean. Half a ton of matter burns in the sky. Aluminium alloy, thermal insulation, copper wire, plastic, rubber, cork. Radio transmitters, control units, batteries. The restraints that confined the dog to her narrow seat, the harness she wore. Instruments, too – that monitored her heart rate, breathing, blood pressure, that conveyed the supply of oxygen was adequate and there was no loss of pressure, that the capsule remained airtight; instruments that confirmed a dog might survive in that enormous vacuum, that it might sit and breathe and eat in a metal container, 600 miles above the earth. Also burning in the sky that night, the remains of the mongrel stray.

Days later, after the woman reads the reports about the light shower, and learns it was the satellite with the dog, she dreams deeply, waking caught beneath the covers, facing the wrong way, the air full of her breath – warm and close, black and still. She remembers a time, years before she met her husband, when she was utterly alone, the skin of her stomach loose from what it had stretched around, from what she had delivered into the world. She recalls the brief weight in her arms, and then the shape of where it had been.

She thinks she will write to her husband about what she saw, certain he will have seen it too. When he returns, he will describe it to her and it will be as if they watched that sky together. She will tell him his mother saw it too, but she will look down as she says this, because it will be hard not to picture the old woman slumped in that fitting room in Robinson's Department Store. Her expression was passive, bland. If she was distressed or upset, she gave nothing away.

* * *

It is 2002, 45 years since a dog was strapped into a capsule and launched into space. In the early evening, south of Perth, Australia, a woman lies on a beach. Her blanket is in the car, her coat and a thermos of coffee too – she was in such a hurry to get along the path. Sand slips down her collar, rubs beneath the cloth of her top. She leans back, allowing a bank of it to shift and cushion her neck.

She comes here every now and again, always after dark when the beach will be empty. There is no particular event that she marks, no anniversary or special occasion. But usually something will have happened, giving rise to an emotional surge – a need to revisit. This time it was the news: *Fate of First Canine Cosmonaut Revealed; Laika's Last Hours*. After all these years. It was on TV first, a current affairs programme. She went online to find out more, but already she knew she'd come here.

During the day this beach is pale and bright, with reddish rocks punctuating the shoreline, water the kind of blue you'd see from space. The sea has pulled away, the surface of the waves glints, catching and reflecting far-off headlamps or porchlights. She never checks the tide – if it's in she keeps to the dunes, but it is better to lie flat, above her the night, its blank black background for the stars like so many grains of sand.

She was twelve when her father first brought her here. Perth was their new home, and on the radio and in the newspapers all the talk was of Sputnik 2 and its living cargo. Television had not yet arrived here but still, you couldn't turn a page or a dial without someone talking rockets or capsules or orbits, that dog and what might follow it into space – the Americans were training monkeys.

They used a map to find the beach. They unfolded it across the bench seat of her father's Holden. He knew the way – this was his boyhood home – but he wanted to teach her to navigate. *How much further south? How long until the turn?* His voice lifted a note at the end of his sentences. He'd sounded out of place when they lived in America, but here everyone spoke like him. Before, her mother had navigated, giving directions with her long vowels and her rounded 'r's, and she sat up front between her parents; they never made her sit in the back. Her father said they were three people who'd found each other, like patches of foam in the sea, joined together, floating as one. Only now they'd buried her mother in her own soil, and there were two oceans and a continent between them. Her disease was hereditary. The woman had always understood why her mother's fate would not be her own – her parents had never made a secret of the explanation. Still, it gave her no comfort.

On the beach, her father opened a bag of iced buns and poured water into picnic cups. They had come to search for the satellite. They would be Moonwatchers, he said – all over the world the

Moonwatchers were sharing sightings, recording coordinates and times, collectively mapping the journey of Sputnik 2. *All we need to do is look up.* Above them, the southern sky with its unfamiliar constellations. She had heard that the Soviets could see the dog on a TV screen, all those miles away in space. But she didn't believe it. Not when she couldn't watch *The Mickey Mouse Club*. She was so far from everything she had known.

If this darkness could sing, it would produce a soft, high-pitched chorus. The woman covers her face with her hands, not yet ready to see. Instead, she listens. No cicadas – it's not warm enough. Somewhere in the dunes a bird calls. Apart from that there is only the sound of her breathing and the waves nuzzling the shore. The sky is swollen; its blackness absorbs the black of the sea. The darkness has blotted away the horizon. Only the stars can transcend this night. The woman shivers, draws her cardigan around her.

On the beach that night, she'd understood in some remote way that her father sought something bigger than his grief and he needed to share it with her. She'd taken one of the little cups, a bun too, biting into it though she didn't feel like eating. The icing was peppered with grit.

Stand up, sweetheart. I think that's it there.

Not wanting to disappoint him, she complied, dropping the remains of the bun.

Can you see it?

No.

She let him turn her head, angling her view and it was as if they were holding tight to each other, carried in a fast-moving current. Her tongue was coated with sugar and sand. Her throat seemed to stick when she swallowed. Everything was moving so quickly. She did not want to let go and be carried forward, but neither could she hold fast to what had been.

I can't see it, Dad.

It's right there. He so badly wanted her to see. *Quick. It'll be gone in a second.*

Yes, I'm looking.

But her neck hurt from the strange tilt of her head, her eyes too, from straining to look anywhere else – at the sand, or out to sea.

I can't see it. She wrenched herself free, pushed him away. *Can't you understand? It's too far.*

She was relieved when the satellite's batteries died a week later. And when the dog was reported dead, she felt nothing. But soon after, she had a peculiar dream, mostly monochrome, but with muted blues and yellows – the colours stayed with her, along with a feeling she carried inside. In the dream, she was seeking a way out of a deep coastal cave, the tide rising, water around her feet, now her thighs, the exit disguised by the encroaching dusk. Every now and again in the years after, the dream would recur. She recognised its approach, the shift in tones, a soft ringing as if her ear was pressed against a seashell.

On the beach, the woman is now ready. It is time to look. When her eyes adjust she identifies the constellations – the Southern Cross, the Alpha Centauri, the phosphorescent Milky Way. Soon enough she sees a light moving among the stars as if making its way along the edge of a crowd, not fast, but constant. She follows it for a moment – it is not a star. It is much closer to the earth – perhaps a communications satellite, or something to do with the weather. Perhaps it is the Space Station. In the north something streaks and disappears. Then, further east, a different satellite jostles its way through the night. Up there are thousands of them: she is in her father's future now. It is as if he has angled her gaze again.

There's nothing there, Dad. I can't see it.

But she did see, as clearly as she can see these lights now, except it was too much to bear then.

In the years after, she collected things with Laika on, perhaps to please her father, but also because she thought herself a kind of stray. Mostly postage stamps – from Mongolia, Albania, Niger. She'd place her finger on the printed ink that marked the journey each had made, across Eastern Europe, Asia, Africa. 1969. 1973. 1981. When the story got into her head, she collected facts too. How Dr Korolev, who designed the rocket, had almost no teeth – all lost during his Siberian exile. How, when the launch was delayed and the dog confined to her narrow space, her keepers warmed her freezing cabin. They lied to their superiors, so they could open up the capsule and give her water. Before the launch, Dr Yazdovsky took Laika home to play with his children. The satellite would not return, he said, so she did not have long to live. He wanted to do something nice for her.

It is 1956. Moscow. A group of dogs are walking, on leads, outside. The sun is shining. There are poplars nearby. Or maybe birches. The leaves shiver lightly, long shadows lie on the grass. One dog is being held by a keeper. She smiles as she rubs its back. Such comforts are a novelty for these animals. Later they will eat, perhaps a soup, with gristle, meal, bone. Any that are being prepared for a test will have extra – bouillon, or even sausage. Dogs that survive a mission can have as much sausage as they want.

Laika takes the place of Albina, whose coat is white, who has recently had pups. A veteran of several sub-orbital flights, Albina is a favourite of the keepers.

The more time passes, the more I'm sorry about it – that was Oleg Gazenko, who selected Laika for the mission. But even when regret is permissible, it does not ease the empty ache.

Some time into the fourth orbit, the telemetry records Laika's agitation: she is barking, she is moving about. In her harness she can stand, or sit, or lie down. There is no room to turn around. The failure of the thermal control; the overheated cabin – an absence of data indicates her death. Seven hours into her journey there is no movement, no record of breathing, though some records claim the trace of a heartbeat, even into the second day. But on November 5th, when the satellite flickers above Rockefeller Plaza, silence.

* * *

New York, 2002. An old man will turn the pages of the *New York Times*. Inside he will see Laika and remember that night on Rockefeller Plaza, the early sky, that tumbling star – her light – and how it seemed to appear and disappear, and when it appeared, how bright it was, the brightest star the newspaper said the next day, brighter than the dog star, Sirius.

The man will doze and dream he is in a tiny capsule, his heart turning over and over, and he will be able to see everything – the smooth arc of the earth's curve, the thin blue mist of its atmosphere, his boys, small again, asleep in their beds, his wife, waiting for him. He will be far away from himself, from the man who stood on the RCA Building searching the night, from the man who abandoned a woman who loved him. He'll be moving at 300 miles a minute, high above the earth, but he will feel as if he is floating, and when he remembers that woman, he will not be afraid.

3ʳᵈ Prize
S. Bhattacharya-Woodward

S. Bhattacharya-Woodward has just completed an MA in Creative and Life Writing at Goldsmiths, University of London. She was shortlisted for the Bridport Short Story Prize in 2018, and longlisted for the Commonwealth Short Story Prize in 2019. She is an award-winning science and health journalist whose articles have featured internationally. She writes for *New Scientist, Nature*, and *BBC Sky at Night* magazine amongst others. She has also contributed to four Dorling Kindersley non-fiction titles and acted as a consultant for television.

Zolo

One foot in front of the other, steady against the wind. Zolo could not look down. He knew if he kept his eyes dead straight on the tops of the other tower blocks he could keep going. One. Two. Three. Gently against the firmness of the concrete, he could keep grounded. He wouldn't fall. There'd be no rush of sirens, nor the excited din of the estate gathering, his mum would never know that her ten-year-old boy had walked the edge of the tower block roof – and not at knifepoint but of his own free will. Worse, what if they thought he'd jumped. *He topped his-self,* that's what they'd say. No way, thought Zolo. They can all go fuck themselves.

He hated heights. At school when he had to walk up two flights of stairs to his classroom, he climbed the stairs on the inside, away from the tall windows on the outer wall of the stairwell. Even then if his eye accidentally caught a glimmer of the sun through the glass, or the thin, high branches of the tree which brushed the window, something in his body swam and he felt he might fall. He didn't let the other kids see. His mum might call him a stupid shit, but he wasn't dumb.

Now, on top of the wall, twenty-five storeys up he didn't just feel the pull of the earth downwards. He felt the familiar tug of the sky.

Sometimes, when he was walking to school, or running through the estate with the other boys he'd feel a lightness, an uneasy pull: the sky was trying to suck him up, into the blue where he'd be lost forever. Don't look up. Zolo would stare at his shoes and the sky would loosen its noose.

Don't look up. Don't look down. Don't step on the cracks. Those are the rules, Zolo reminded himself. Just keep going.

The edges of the roof were raised concrete, a metre thick and a metre high. The people who walked the wall were mostly nutters or psychos, or a combination of the two. When the teenagers did it, they showed-off – one palm on the concrete and then a kind of jump with two feet onto the wall, as if they were skateboarding or something. At least that's what Spider Syd, CJ, and Kaz from the maisonettes, did.

For kids Zolo's age, walking the inside of the wall's perimeter was enough to show you weren't a wimp. When he did that the first time, the block boys' eyes on him, Zolo held his breath and stomach tightly. He walked the four inside walls, staring rigidly at the floor, one hand groping wallside; reached his start point and vomited, the jeers and yelps mixing with the sounds of his body's gurgles and retches.

This time, no one was watching. And this time, he was on top of the wall, one skinny, tin-pot rail about ten centimetres high and a ruler-length from the edges, between him and the sheer drop. Zolo had pulled himself up on one corner of the tower's large, rectangular roof. He put one hand firm on each wall and hoisted himself over the broken bottles, fast food boxes and the small metal canisters emptied of laughing gas, that the teenagers had thrown away; holding his breath to steady himself against his fear, and to block out the wafting smells of urine mixed with fried chicken.

As he sat on the corner, the grey blocks and green strips of the estate falling away on either side, dizziness hit him. A shockwave travelling from the distant ground, right up, higher, higher, higher – till bang. In the face. Zolo took a moment to steady himself. Closed his eyes. Don't look. Whatever you do. Don't look down. Then he had opened his eyes straight ahead, raised one knee, then the other. And stood.

From the solid corner of the concrete roof, Zolo stood and placed one foot in front of the other. That's all it is. One foot. Then the other. One foot. Then the other.

His stomach settled. He was halfway across the first wall when a pigeon flew straight past, shaving close to his face, to land in the fast food boxes in the corner. Zolo's body tilted so slightly backwards; a small stick on the top of the tall tower that swayed a minuscule one degree, two degrees, backwards as the pigeon whizzed in front of his eyes. It was enough to see the mangy brown feathers that tapered to dirty white against the wide sky. Enough to feel the world tilt.

Zolo's body swayed forwards an inch, recalibrated itself. He felt sick. And annoyed. He glanced sideways at the flat concourse of the roof and saw the pigeon ambling back across, half a thin chip in its beak. Zolo wanted to kick it. His leg wanted to go forwards towards the bird, like little kids do. Like Zakky used to do. Chasing pigeons like a mini footballer with stumpy legs and a big nappy, yelping when the pigeons finally upped and moved a metre away and continued with whatever they were doing, nonplussed.

Now the toddler sat all day, belted into his buggy facing the wall of his mum's bedroom. He didn't cry anymore. Just sat with a blank, tired look on his face. Zakky's dad left. Mum didn't want anything to do with the baby. 'You change his nappy then if you're so bothered,' she told Zolo. 'Turn the buggy round and see his dad's ugly mug? No, he's right as rain.'

Big Ray came round. He wasn't big. More average. He was only called Big Ray on account of there being a Little Ray years before in their class at Clearbrook Field Primary. Zolo's mum and Big Ray stayed in for days, the walls of the flat slowly staining with smoke, bottles piling up by the sofa. They lived in the 'penthouse' as his mum called it, right there at the top of the tower. Zolo was okay inside, he just never went too close to the windows or stood on the balcony if he could help it. But with Zakky facing the wall, and mum and Big Ray not moving in the living room, Zolo had to sort things. He'd had enough of going to school with stinking clothes; kids pinching their noses and pelting small, hard rectangles of soap from the school toilets at him. He washed his uniform in the bathroom sink and edged onto the balcony. He'd tell himself the bars around the balcony would keep him safe. He wouldn't fall. He shut his eyes and felt for the plastic washing line that went lengthways across the balcony's narrow middle as he hung up his wet school shirt and trousers.

He'd give Zakky a bottle. Sometimes he'd mash the baby a banana the way his mum used to. He'd lump it onto a plastic baby spoon and raise it to Zakky's mouth, but the baby would turn his face away and strain his belted body sideways. Zolo turned the baby's buggy round once, at the beginning when he was still screaming, but his mum had come in heavily from behind him with a sharp jolt to the small of Zolo's back. He tried to change the baby's nappies, he remembered how Zakky's dad did it, but the baby was sore and screaming, and Zolo could only manage it now and again.

Then the electric went off. Big Ray had left by then. 'Mum, get the electric.' But Zolo's mum buried her head deeper into the sofa. 'Give me the money then and I'll go to the shop and charge the key.' She didn't answer and there was nothing in her bag.

Days went by and the smell started. A low, slightly nauseous hum at first. But after several more days, and a sudden summer heat that seemed to raise steam from the estate's concrete bones and strip the tops of men and boys to skins, the smell was beyond anything Zolo could have imagined. You choked in it. Your lungs deflated trying to squeeze every bit of the poison out and yet breathe at the same time. It wiped out all hunger. The rancour of rotting meat.

The smell spilled from the fridge, to the kitchen, to the whole flat. A noxious, invisible mist; it began to seep from under the door, out into the shared corridor, past the neighbours' doors and to the lifts.

'Come here,' Mrs C from next door beckoned as Zolo waited for the lifts. 'What's that smell?' She took a deep drag on her cigarette. Flecks of ash fell onto her patterned nylon shirt, before tumbling to the ground.

'Dunno,' said Zolo, watching the dying motes fall, and staring at flat, black circles of gum stuck to the floor where they landed.

'I haven't seen Zakky for a while,' she said, waving her cigarette smoke with a gnarled hand over the stench like perfume.

Zolo shrugged and walked towards the door of the stairwell.

Social Services called round later that day. A greying, lank man with trainers and a hard face. Zolo thought social workers were supposed to look kind, to children at least. 'It was you, wasn't it? You fucking grassed,' his mum's eyes bulged afterwards. 'I never,' said Zolo. And she went for him.

After that Zolo knew the sky would suck him up for sure. He could feel invisible strings like comic-book zaps coming at him when he was out-of-doors, unprotected, outside. And he knew he had to find a way to control it. To make it all right. He had to front it out. That's when he knew he had to walk the wall.

Zolo got to the first corner, broad and sharp against the sky. He felt his chest expand. He could breathe. Now turn.

The view changed, the same grey rectangles and green lines fell below, but look straight ahead and past the tops of the other towers and there in the hazy distance were the gleaming pinnacles of the City. He tried to focus, but his attention drifted out towards the glass skyscrapers in their improbable shapes: concave; convex, skinny in the middle and flaring out at the top; sharp and pointy. Could you walk those? Probably not – there didn't look like there were any flat parts to their tops. But if you could. If you could. You'd be Superman.

Maybe Spider Syd could? Spider Syd (otherwise called Syeed) had long, thin legs and equally spindly arms. He lived in one of the seven-storey blocks next to Zolo's high-rise. A daredevil from a young age, Syd was legendary among the kids of the estate; rushing up his block's central stairwell to his cousin's flat at the top of the building. There he would appear on the balcony and dangling off the side rails, would hang-drop level to level. The kids would gather at the bottom, while he gracefully pulled his body taut and hung and swung his way down seven floors of the building; landing with a balletic backflip over brambles and onto grass verge to whoops and some jeers (no one likes a show-off), and a healthy dose of swearing from the residents whose balconies he'd breached.

When Spider Syd had walked the wall, it was for no other reason than he really was a show-off. Zolo imagined he was Syd. But he couldn't muster Syd's cocky ease. Instead the gleaming buildings were calling him. Calling him to look. To drift over the blue sky to dreams built of brilliant glass.

And Zolo *was* drifting. Up and up. A helium balloon let go by Zakky in the days when his dad was still around, and mum still loved

Zakky; buying him candy floss, and a Mickey Mouse-shaped balloon when the sorry excuse for a fairground (three faded rides, an unscary ghost train, a couple of stalls) set up on the wiry grass of the local park on the bank holiday weekend. Zolo saw Zakky's mouth ringed pink and grainy with strands of wet candy floss.

Drifting, Zolo's body forgot itself. Three-quarters of the way across the second wall, it was as if he suddenly awoke and did not know where he was. The steadiness in his body unfurled and he was a paper cut-out boy swaying in the wind. Focus. Focus. One foot. Then the other. One foot. Then the other. Nausea hit Zolo as the solidity of his body seemed to melt away. No. Fix on one thing. One thing. He steadied his gaze. And breathed slowly in and out. In and out. His stomach settled and he felt the firm reality of the concrete wall through his trainers. He made it to the end of the second wall.

Turning on the second corner, Zolo wished it were over. He knew he had to do it. But would it work? Tomorrow, the grey social worker would be back with his colleague, and they would look and judge and decide. When the Social had come round, Zolo's mum thought quickly on her feet and said she'd been too ill to go out and top up the electric, but she was well again now and yes everything was all right, the baby was like that because he'd been ill too, and he felt comfy in his buggy.

Zolo's mum had topped up the electric and cleaned the flat. She'd emptied the fridge, a cloth tied in a triangle around her mouth and nose like a cowboy in an old Western. With armfuls of kitchen towel she'd soaked up the putrid liquids pooling in the base of the fridge and in the plastic vegetable trays. She scrubbed and sprayed and sprayed and scrubbed. She used a whole can of air freshener until only a faint murmur of rotting flesh was left in the air behind a heavy veil of White Linen.

She'd cleaned Zakky. She took him out of the buggy, bathed him, gave him a fresh nappy and clean clothes. But Zakky had looked limp. His eyes glassy; not like the beautiful, shining glass of the skyscrapers, but like small marbles set in sockets. He went back and sat in the buggy of his own accord, his thin hands hanging by his sides.

Zolo kept going. He told himself he was past halfway and he just needed to do the same again. His stomach was getting used to the height. If he looked straight ahead he could trick his mind so it felt neither the pull of the sky, nor of the ground. You could get used to anything really.

The third corner. Zolo felt a different feeling in his gut now. A bubbling – not nausea – something rising, something powerful like hope without the placidity of hope. It was restless and fiery. He hadn't known this sensation before. It told him that he would do it. He would make it all the way round. He placed his feet carefully, but more resolutely now. If he had looked to the side, he might have seen a few people, like ants moving around at the base of the tower, slowly gathering. But he kept on. Zolo was now steps away from his goal.

Three. Two. One. Home.

Zolo stood on that final corner. A small boy on a tall tower. He closed his eyes and felt the sun on his lids and the blowing wind soft on his face. He had done it. He was all right. He didn't know what would happen tomorrow. Whether they would stay or be taken away. But right then, it didn't matter.

He opened his eyes and sat slowly down on the concrete corner. Cross-legged at first, he uncurled his right leg, then his left, hooking them over the low, thin rail and dangled them over the precipice. One leg either side of the hard corner. Above a falling world.

Rua Breathnach

Rua Breathnach was born in Dublin, where he grew up and attended school and university. He is the author of two one-act plays, *Rondo* and *Avenida* (published in one volume by Editions Bomarzo, Brussels), and the critically-acclaimed play, *Welcome to the Stranger*, which premiered at Skibbereen Arts Festival in 2018. He lives in Ghent, Belgium, with his wife and two daughters. *The Bridge* is his first published story.

The Bridge

I f we want to go back, we'll have to go way back, to a beginning, to a time before I was born, to a boy and a girl, both seventeen years of age, crossing a bridge over the Glenamoy River, in winter, with, as the saying goes, "everything they own on their backs"; with, that is, the very little they possess: the rough leather boots, the thick-cut cloth, the shawl and starched linen, the woolen underwear, still damp and smelling of turf smoke, the few pounds for the passage to America; the girl's fresh face, the boy's determined jaw, their hobnailed footsteps ringing on the cast-iron bridge. But this would be cheating. There are no photographs, no dear diaries, no lock of hair coiled inside a silver pendant; no history, in fact, only the bridge and the bones of a story my father told me one summer afternoon as we sat in the upstairs room of our house, above his dental practice, in Philadelphia, when I was a girl.

Ours was a tall redbrick house on Carlisle Street, just two blocks from Rittenhouse Square. In my mind's eye I am always approaching it from the same angle; a long row of houses is interrupted by an overgrown lot, and there it is – the side wall, windowless at street level, with an enclosed balcony on the second floor. I approach it now, seeking an earlier incarnation of myself. It is the beginning of the summer vacation; my mother and my older sister, Margaret, have just left for the country, and I am alone in the house with Papa.

I can see the upstairs room clearly – the floorboards covered with a faded rug, the fireplace with the broken clock as its centerpiece, the coal box, bellows and two stiff-backed armchairs – not surprising, considering the amount of time I must have spent there keeping my father company on his lunchbreaks; though I'm no longer convinced he was always present as we sat together listening to his favorite records. I'm not so sure because now I can recall, on more than one occasion, the music running out, the needle stuck in the final groove, producing a hollow, regular thud. In my mind's eye, my father's head is tilted, his face toward the ceiling and his mouth open. Asleep in the chair, he has become one of his patients, paralyzed in the moment before the drill begins to whine. In his hand, nestled in his lap, is a heavy-bottomed glass, recently half-full. He wakes to find his daughter tugging on his sleeve.

— Papa, papa… Maggie wouldn't let me ride with her and Mama in the car.

— What time is it? Are they gone?

Straightening himself up, he leans over and places the whiskey tumbler on the small table at his elbow.

— I was dreaming. I was dreaming in Gaelic. Isn't that a strange thing?

I'm crying.

He pats his lap.

— Sit down with me a minute. There, that's better. Ah, don't be crying now. Imagine you are flying solo across the Atlantic…

About three miles outside Bangor, where a stand of Scots pine marks the turnoff on the Belmullet road, as if to warn the driver she is encroaching on a new geography, a gust jolts the Renault Clio firmly to the center of the road. At the Texaco gas station, the attendant advised to "fill up the tank as there's no pump now at Glenamoy." The rain, when it comes, spits on the windshield, then bursts in a torrent and drums on the hood and roof. Wiping a porthole, she presses her face toward the glass, the car lurching across the blanket bog like a beetle in a hailstorm.

Sadie is at the door as the car comes to a halt before the gate of the bungalow. She is wearing a dress, a soft cotton apron tied about the waist. For the occasion, she has clipped up her slate-gray hair and dabbed her thin mouth with lipstick. It's only the clunky leather boots that give her away as a farmer's widow more accustomed to feeding chickens than entertaining American visitors. Kate opens the gate and walks up the footpath wheeling her suitcase behind her. The two women embrace. As they step into the hallway, Sadie opens the door to the guest room and deposits Kate's luggage inside. The visitor is ushered into the parlor, a small room at the front of the house where a turf fire is burning.

— Sit there quietly and warm yourself up while I see to the dinner.

Sadie shuffles out of the room, leaving the door ajar.

The hearth is papered over with imitation brickwork. In a corner, a cabinet displays glassware and, sitting on the top, a plastic bottle molded in the shape of the Virgin Mary. Beside the Virgin is a framed photograph of Sadie on her wedding day, squinting (or perhaps smiling) into the sunshine.

The front door is pushed open. Heavy boots clump up the hallway. A few words are muttered at the kitchen door. Kate puts back the photograph, her body tensing. The boots clump back down the hallway and the door swings open. The two adults stand face to face, Kate still wearing her raincoat and Tom in a pair of dirty jeans tucked into rubber boots and a sweater with a lozenge-pattern down the front.

— Hullo, Kate.

She steps forward and they shake hands.

— Hiya, Tom. Good to see you. You haven't changed a bit.

In the cramped kitchen, Sadie serves a meal of pork chops, peas, and potatoes, all swimming in a pool of gravy. The conversation is not so much awkward as in danger of being swallowed by one of the long silences Kate tries to fill with a series of questions. Sadie, bustling around the kitchen, pauses after each question, wiping her fingers in her apron.

— We've only the three hens left. The cows were sold to Francy Gallagher. Ah, a long while back. Poor Francy is dead since. Of old age. The O'Tooles were always very good to him and he left them the land.

Tom bolts his food, the joints of his chair cracking as he shifts his weight.

— Oh, there were very few cars back then. I used to walk the three miles to Rossport, pick up the groceries at Dinny's, and walk the three miles back. Tom gives me a lift to Belmullet now on a Friday. And the traveling shop comes around on Tuesday evenings. For small things.

When the dishes are washed, dried, and put away, the dishcloths hung to dry over the stove, and three places set for the morning, Kate kisses the old woman on the cheek and, fetching her toilet bag from her suitcase, locks herself in the bathroom. Perched on the side of the bathtub brushing her teeth, the brownish water trickling from the faucet into the washbowl, it comes back to her: the mid-August heatwave, the half-acres dotted with haycocks, the sunburnt men in rolled-up shirtsleeves with pitchforks in their hands, stooping and rising. Sadie and herself carrying flasks of tea and corned-beef sandwiches down to the men in the fields; the men speaking Gaelic, barely looking up as she passes to pour them the tea.

She wakes early. The murmur of a radio comes from behind a closed door at the end of the hall opposite the kitchen. Sadie is standing over the stove frying eggs and slices of bacon. She turns around and smiles faintly as Kate puts her hand on her shoulder.

— Morning. Smells good.

The two women eat in silence. Finishing her tea, Kate picks up a pair of binoculars from the windowsill beside the table and, adjusting the focus, scans the hill.

— I think I'll go up to the house.

Sadie is staring at her empty plate streaked with egg yolk, her hands in her lap.

— *Teach Sonny*, Kate says, putting down the binoculars.

Sadie nods, smiling at the use of the Gaelic name for Kate's father's house – the house that was never built, that was already a ruin before the first stone was laid in the boggy ground Sadie's father sold him.

Kate puts on her raincoat and hiking boots and, slinging a Kodak over her shoulder, sets off across the low, rushy ground to the foot of the hill. The torrents have cut deep gashes into the hillside; whole sections of stony earth have broken away and lie tumbled across the path. Sheep with blue and pink markings give her a wide berth as she clambers over the debris. At the point where the grazing gives way to open heath, the path joins a paved road that veers off and offers a view westward over the narrow channel with its horseshoe beach.

The plot of land is much smaller than she remembers it. In the northeast corner, two whitethorns hunch their backs against the prevailing winds. A shallow stream runs through a culvert under the road and marks the seaward boundary of the land. Standing near the roadside is a square shed, its corrugated-metal roof weighed down with tires and large stones secured with rope.

After her mother divorced her father, this was the fantasy that sustained him through his last years: he would return, set up a dental practice in Belmullet, tend sheep and cut turf, connect the house to the grid. He had drawn up the blueprints and obtained the building permit. He had considered every square inch of his tiny plot and was convinced the plan was viable. It all worked on paper and it would all work in reality. Tom and herself had come up here for a picnic in '67; had lain a blanket in the long grass protected from the nibbling sheep by a dry-stone wall.

As she picks her way downhill, stopping every now and then to take in the view and snap a few pictures, she sees Tom approaching from below, a sheepdog at his heels. This is the same path up which they drove Snake and Roberts more than thirty years ago; Kate carrying a switch, and Tom running alongside crying *"drish, drish!"* to prevent the cows from straying too near the edge.

When he's a few yards away, she can see that he is completely winded.

— Hey, there. I was up at the plot. You've done great work keeping out the livestock.

Tom takes off his cap, doubles over, and puts his hands on his thighs to catch his breath.

— I'd be more worried about keeping out the O'Tooles.

— They won't be too happy to see I've been snooping around then.

— Ah, bugger the lot of them! Isn't it your own land?

He turns and spits over the side of the path.

In all this time he has not once looked her in the eye, but now turns directly to face her. His gray eyes set in a bony peasant's face stare up into her own, also gray but flecked with blue.

— Mam was wondering if you're coming in for your tea.

— I was on my way down.

— And will you be staying long?

She pauses.

— No, not this time. I've rented the car and...

— I understand your wanting to get out of this place.

Turning, he indicates the valley with his cap.

— I didn't mean that. I know your mother will be disappointed, it's just...

— She's very shook. I'm not sure she knows where she's at most of the time.

— I know, and it can't be easy for you, either.

— I'll be alright, Kate. At this stage in my life, I'm past having illusions.

The next morning, at the gate, I say goodbye to them both. Sadie, stiff in my arms, clings as we kiss. Tom, cursing, holds the unruly dog by the collar, his gray eyes distant again.

The door of the car slams shut and I roll down the window.

— It's a fine day for traveling, Sadie says, looking up at the sky.

I start up the engine, shift the gear lever into drive and, releasing the brake, press my foot on the accelerator.

Gaining speed slowly, the car just about clears the telephone lines at the end of the narrow road and lifts up and over the horseshoe beach.

Out over the Atlantic I'm free, and I no longer care nor need to know what has become of the stone walls Tom so diligently preserved in my father's absence.

Maybe they hoped he would come back and settle; maybe they knew it was all a dream; maybe Sadie still loved him and maybe Tom was my half-brother and that's why my father cut the trip in '67 short, when he saw us getting too close.

I only know what he told me: They parted on the bridge that winter morning, and he watched Sadie slowly trace her path back along the frozen road, never once turning, her shawl wrapped tightly about her head – back to the past, as he called it, back to where we all come from.

Sabah Carrim

Sabah Carrim has authored two novels, *Humeirah* and *Semi-Apes*. Both stories are set in Mauritius where she was born. Sabah's short stories have been selected for publication in writing competitions organised by the Commonwealth Foundation and Goethe Institute South Africa. At the 2019 African Writers Conference in Kenya, Sabah delivered the keynote address on *Cultural Stereotypes in African Literature*. She will also be attending the Aké Arts and Book Festival in Nigeria for the launch of an anthology containing one of her short stories. Sabah is a Genocide Scholar, a law lecturer, and currently lives in Kuala Lumpur.

The Evil in Me

If you want to convince someone that you've locked her up and there's no escape, would it be better to place a bigger padlock on the door instead of a smaller one?

Madina – 1422 al hijra /2001 anno domini

In a van with tinted windows, driven by a man whose face I can't see, I'm taken far away from the haram shareef where I've prayed and visited the tomb of the Prophet for the first time in my life.

When they slide open the door of the vehicle, I'm told I'm in the middle of a date field, but it isn't a proper field like the sugarcane field behind my house: Bursts of flared-green in mud-brown against a blue sky of cloudy symbols, where the silence that reigns is blessed by freshness, youth, naïvety, and has hope – a future.

No. Where I stand, the land is barren, sandy, desolate; the date trees thorny, cactus-like, with husks protruding eerily, hiding scorpions, blades, snakes, and centipedes that can sting you like a jab of poison, that can rob you of your middle finger.

Every feature of the landscape seems to have been bleached by the sun, sucked of its juices by the heat; mean, vindictive, and yet inert, like the deceptive eyes of an iguana. This is nothing but gloom and depression laid out through a film of varied grey. The silence here is aged: not wise and dignified but pained, strained and morbid, as if recovering from war, the plague, a long disease. Chillies could certainly never grow here.

This is the first time I'm seeing a date tree, or so many date trees in such a vast expanse of land. My husband has brought me on pilgrimage to Makkah and Madina to rid me of evil. But praying at the haram shareef five times a day, circumambulating the Kaaba seven times, drinking water from The Well of Zamzam in three breaths, aren't enough, he says. He said Taufik-said more must be done for it to work, and none of what's about to happen he cautioned, has ever been mentioned in the books.

The hut I'm led to in the date field is plain, ordinary and rustic, stripped of all forms and manners of perfection. I'm shoved into a dark room, and notice that what separates me from the outside is a padlock that covers half the door: it's the biggest I've ever seen in my life.

Then I realise I'm not alone: women in black abayas and niqaabs invade the emptiness around me. I can feel our shoulders touching, our arms, the rest of our bodies. I no longer feel myself, I'm turned into a shapeless form, merging into this black flow of sameness.

Someone throws a bucket of water on me. (Later I'm told it's Holy water.) I'm in a state of shock, I burst into loud sobs realising I'm bare, naked, exposed because they can see me, my face, my eyes, my identity; they can see how I am struggling with the evil in me, and yet I can't see them, their expressions, whether they feel anything for me, or understand, because their black eyes are veiled with black netting.

The loudspeakers in the room sound chants, loud chants in Arabic I can't recognise. I don't know what's going on.

Then I begin to see insects, strange insects, straw-like, cricket-like coming out of nowhere, from underneath the single pink bin placed before me, ready for when I want to throw up. (How could they know that?). The insects travel over me at different speeds, some with their thousand feet, others with slimy bodies, over my neck, my chest, my thighs, my face. I can't breathe, nor move; I feel hot, restrained, suffocated. No one will hear me even if I cry for help. What's happening is wrong, so wrong, but how can I explain it, and even if I find the words, who'll understand?

I collapse onto the ground. *Les mwa trankil* – Leave me alone... *Fer mwa sorti depi la* – Get me out of here...

My father always spoke highly of the caretaker at school. I was eight at that time, and I reckoned it was because a caretaker takes care. A caretaker takes-care. Acaretakertakescare.

My father worked long hours, that's why he was never on time to pick me up from school. The government held him back: he had to stand guard as a policeman when parliament was in session. The school caretaker, whom I called Nana – grandfather, would look after me for an hour or so. He would speak to the hawker who sold sweets to the children outside the gate (the Headteacher kept telling us not to buy anything from him) and ask him for one or two *salangi* – sweet and sour dried plums I liked so much. The hawker must have been scared of Nana because he did what he was told.

Sometimes it was boring to be in the schoolyard so Nana would hold my hand and walk me to the garden in Plaine Verte. He would make me sit next to him on a bench, and when passers-by would ask if I was his granddaughter, he would smile and nod and say, Yes, she's like my granddaughter. When they would move away, he would slip his hand into mine and place it under the school bag on his lap.

Sometimes I felt the wetness, sometimes I didn't. But it always grew big and hard. He asked me if I had my menses, and I always said no because I didn't know what he meant. He would breathe heavily in my ear, whispering anecdotes of how girls I knew at school had asked to be touched. He told me that while watching a sexually explicit movie at Cinema Rex, an attractive girl had come up to him, offered to light up his cigarette, and had asked him to do certain things to her – I remember that cinema very well, because it was the same one where on Saturdays my father would take me to watch funny movies by Louis de Funès.

I don't know, I can't help it, I keep wondering whether the evil came into me because of all the time I spent with Nana on the bench after school.

Go to your kitchen and look for the bottle of olive oil. Pick it up and examine its contents. Do you see any bubbles? Because if you do, please throw the bottle away. And don't unscrew the top, just don't open it.

They say the *mannat* – special prayer didn't work. I'm at the house of my in-laws in Port Louis. They say it's better for me to be with them because they pray regularly, and are therefore more protected from the evil than I am in my house all by myself, where I would most likely skip my prayers – And evil is drawn to women who don't have the protection of men.

First I'm taken to see the imaam in the masjid of Vallée des Prêtres, and he says the only way out is to send me for counselling. But my husband says that counselling-and-all-that is a western method and won't solve the problem. Instead, he remembers his school friend Dr. R – who specialises in endocrinology and studied medicine in an English university. When we go and see him and tell him about how I've been misbehaving, and about the evil in me, he confirms that what's happening is beyond the reach of western medicine. There is no other solution but to try something different. My husband is satisfied with the answer, and seems to know what he means. Here is a Muslim brother who understands, he says, as we drive back to the house.

Taufik and a few other imaams are to come in the evening between Asr and Maghrib to do another round of *ruqyat* – incantation. I've been forbidden to mention Taufik's name to my friends and relatives because he's wanted by the police for a murder he swears he hasn't committed. I've been told that when the arrest warrant was issued, he escaped to Madina, and won a scholarship there to study Islam. Now he's back, but illegally, and no one knows that.

Taufik brings a senior imaam, a *maulana* with him to perform the ritual. My head is sprayed with Holy water, and the five men who are seated on the carpet next to me are reciting Arabic verses I don't recognise. The maulana taps my feet with a broom because that is the point of exit where the evil will come out. Nothing happens. Then he comes to me and squeezes my neck until I can't breathe, all the while reassuring my husband and our relatives that the only way to communicate with the jinn is to deprive me of oxygen. My voice turns grave and scruffy, and when I cry out to them to leave me alone, I start sounding like a man. The maulana looks up at everyone with his hand still clasping my neck, and tells them this is the jinn manifesting itself. He asks the evil in me to speak, and it does, and says it got inside my body through the food I ate at Sarawasti's house. *Kari pwason ek brinzel* – Fish curry with brinjal.

It says it used to live happily in a dark cave with its wife; that one day it was suddenly sucked out of it and aspirated into my body and has been trapped in me ever since. Then I hear myself laughing, shouting, making predictions, telling everyone the icebergs will melt, the world will be swallowed up by water, fire, earthquakes, people will do wrong, the Mahdi will appear, that Qayamat – the End is near. I'm also pronouncing words I've never heard myself utter before. The maulana turns to the others and says I'm speaking Malgache, the dialect of Madagascar. Many jinns come from there, he continues. He speaks to the evil in me, and commands it to turn over a new leaf by reading the Shahadah and converting to Islam. He tries to woo the jinn by telling it that if it converts, food will be plentiful, as Muslims do sacrifices regularly, so there will always be enough animal carcasses to feed on. (I'm told later that jinns live on bones).

Then the maulana puts his palm on my shaved head (I was asked to shave it before the ritual), and digs into it with his nails. His hand moves all around my scalp, and I'm crying out in pain. I'm sure it must be bleeding by now. He keeps saying he has caught the jinn, that it has got away, and moves around my scalp pinching it again and again.

Finally, he says he has managed to catch it. He holds something invisible between his thumb and forefinger, and Taufik hands him a bottle of olive oil. He unscrews it and the maulana deposits the invisible thing into it. Quickly, he closes the cap. See, I caught him, Alhamdulillah, he tells my husband, Do you see the bubble inside?

My husband peers into the bottle and says, Alhamdulillah, yes, I see it, maulana, I see it.

And everyone cries out in chorus: Alhamdulillah, Alhamdulillah, Alhamdulillah.

Long before I was born, the newspaper reported that a 24 year-old was traipsing somewhere in Port Louis when men accosted him, beat him up and one of them held his hand on the ground and said: Tell me, which finger? Which finger did you use to do what you did?

When there was no reply, he produced a blade and sliced off the man's middle finger.

One day, there was a wedding in the family and only the Misters and Missuses were invited. My parents weren't close to their relatives, so my father had the idea of leaving me with Nana.

I remember that day clearly. How could I not? It was a Sunday, and my father dropped me off at Nana's house. I had never been there before. There was a big courtyard and many small houses all around, painted in different colours: bright red, bright green, bright blue, bright pink, bright orange. No one seemed to be around. I remember examining the potted plants that decorated the exteriors of all the houses, especially the one next to Nana's house. Nana reassured my father that there was nothing to worry about, and that he would drop me back on time. When my father left, Nana let me play with an old Shape Sorting Box. Most of the pieces, I remember, were missing.

After a while Nana drew the curtains of all the windows, turned the key in the main door, and came and sat next to me. He asked me whether I had my menses, and as usual I said no. Then he lifted me up and took me to the dining table, made me stand on top of it, and took off my panties. Turn by turn, he dug each finger of his right hand into me, including the middle one, especially the middle one, the one that was merely a stub.

Stub, Finger, Finger, Finger, Thumb. Stub, Finger, Finger, Finger, Thumb.

I remember how his eyes were closed, and I remember the facial hair that had grown haphazardly around his lips and chin. In some places, the little hairs were white and still stuck to his skin, in others, especially on his chin, they were much longer, irregular in shape, size, thickness; some white, some grey, some black. Frizzy hairs that I would always remember whenever I would watch the TV commercial:

Wella Wellastrate, Hair Straightening Cream (Intense)
In the last frame of the commercial, the white cap of the long tube of Wella Wellastrate would catch a frizzy hair and twirl it round and round, until it would gradually become straight.
Stub, Finger, Finger, Finger, Thumb.

When I turned eighteen, my mother wanted to teach me about marriage. She said that imaam-said: A man must take care of a woman, that's why there's marriage. A husband must take care of his wife.
It made me realise that a husband is his wife's caretaker. A caretaker takes-care. Acaretakertakescare. A husband takes care.

That's why I decided to fall in love with a man. And when we did it, I told him about my fear that I would never be able to get married again, because no one would accept a girl who was no longer a virgin. It seems that that was why he decided to marry me. (At least, that's what he said afterward.)

Everything went on as planned. On the night of our wedding however, I turned him down when he approached me because I could not stand the beard he had grown. He said he had wanted to hide the bout of acne that had recently erupted on his face. When he asked why I didn't like his beard, I wasn't sure, but I replied, It's ugly... It reminds me of...of...

(and I thought of something disgusting so he would understand)...of pubic hair.

The following day, my husband shaved his beard. When we finally did it, there was no amputated-middle-finger, and there was no need for chickens pecking on ivory and purple coloured chillies.

But there was a lot of disappointment.

Three chickens in a courtyard. Pecking ivory chillies, purple chillies, chillies I've never seen before. Chillies it seems, you see only once in your life.

In the house with Nana, as I said, I was standing on the dining table and my panties had been taken off. Stub, Finger, Finger, Finger, Thumb. Then Nana lifted me again, and took me into a bedroom. He placed me in his bed and rolled my dress up to my chest. Stub, Finger, Finger, Finger, Thumb. With a reassuring smile, he undid his belt, pulled out his trousers and his underwear, and lay down next to me.

That's when there was a knock on the door. Nana asked me to pull up my panties while he quickly slipped on his underwear and trousers. It was the khala from next door. She was complaining that Nana's chickens were eating the chillies from the pots in front of her house. She was frantic, and kept saying they were chillies that were rarely found at the market, and took a long time to grow. I remembered them. They were the ivory and purple coloured chillies I had seen in the plant pots before I entered Nana's house.

Then the khala saw me, and asked Nana whose daughter I was, and what I was doing there. Nana gave all the right answers and once he got all his chickens into their cages, he came back inside. He said it was time to leave, and walked me back to my house.

A few days later I told my mother what Nana had said: something about a white cream that could come out if he was happy. My mother must have spoken to my father about it, because I never saw Nana again. My parents never asked what happened, and anyway, I didn't mind it, because when I look back now, I realise I wouldn't have had the words to express myself.

As I said earlier, my father worked as a policeman, but not the ordinary fearless policeman everyone imagines one to be. He was a fearful policeman who didn't want to get into trouble, and a fearful policeman who would do anything to not lose his job. Because one day, many years later, haunted by my past, by those memories with Nana, I lay in bed crying, and my father who knew why, walked into my bedroom and shouted: What can I do? What do you want me to do? Kill him?

That's why after that, I never let them see me cry. But by keeping all those emotions hidden inside, I think that's how I may have attracted the evil in me.

Relapse:
noun
ˈrē ˌlaps/
A deterioration in someone's state of health after a temporary improvement.

The ruqyat with the maulana and Taufik hasn't worked. That's why I've had a relapse and I'm meeting Sarawasti again. Sarawasti is sixteen years old and she's one of my students at school. I'm in love with her. Before I got married, she invited me to her house, and her mother prepared a meal for us: *kari pwason ek brinzel* – Fish curry with brinjal. It was delicious. Then we took a long walk hand in hand by the beach in Pointe aux Piments. But Sarawasti and I broke up before I got married.

Then after a few years, we got in touch again. She started coming home often. One day my husband caught us at it, and of course he was enraged. I told him the truth: that I have always been drawn to women, not men, and that I couldn't help it. We sat down and dug for reasons for my misbehaviour and sinful nature, and could only think of Nana, and what he had done.

Let me try to remember everything... Let me try to recollect what has happened to me so far.

Yes, my husband insisted on knowing everything about Sarawasti, so I told him about the meal her mother had lovingly prepared, the walk on the beach... He told me that along the beach in Pointe aux Piments, people do prayers, and maybe that's how the evil must have come into me. He made me undergo a few sessions of exorcism, then took me to a Muslim psychiatrist who listened to us and said I was suffering from Gender Identity Disorder, or Gender Confusion. It seems I was confused about my gender. It made sense at first, but I told her later on that I couldn't help being confused by my gender, and she suggested that I was probably suffering from DID – Dissociative Identity Disorder, or MPD – Multiple Personality Disorder.

That was when Abdullah manifested himself. Yes.

Abdullah was that part of me that loved women, only women... It made so much sense... A split personality, made of me and of Abdullah.

Abdullah liked to dress in men's clothes, felt more comfortable wearing boxer shorts, men's shoes, men's trousers, men's shirts. My husband said Abdullah was the name of the evil jinn in me, and during one of the rituals of exorcism that followed, he eventually identified himself as such.

This was then. After that visit to the Muslim psychiatrist, my husband took me to the imaam in Vallée des Prêtres, Dr R – the endocrinologist, and then to Taufik who arranged for that trip to Makkah and Madina, followed by the ritual with the maulana.

Now that I have reconciled myself to accepting who I am, who I can't help being, my husband has grown more and more uneasy at home. He has mentioned divorce many times, but his parents have advised against it, because Divorce Should Only Be A Last Resort.

My husband brought another man recently, after discounting the healing abilities of the maulana. This time it was a different maulana – Maulana Bahadoor, a man known to do rituals of protection after business hours in some of the shops selling cloth in Port Louis. His diagnosis was that the evil came into me because my great-grandparents had made A Pact With The Devil to enrich themselves, but had not fulfilled their part of the promise. That was why, he said, I had become the sacrificial victim.

Maulana Bahadoor suggested that our names – Sarawasti and mine – be written on eggshells, then advised my husband to bury them in the middle of the night in an abandoned grave in the cemetery of Riche Terre.

But even that, it seems hasn't worked.

My only solace is what I learnt in catechism classes at school (yes, my parents allowed me to attend those, but my husband suspects that that may be how the evil came into me):

Let him who is without sin cast the first stone.

I've decided I can't help it. I can't help being drawn to Sarawasti, to women, their soft skin, their breasts, their beautiful bodies, their smooth hair, their legs, what's in between. I understand women's bodies and women's emotions better than I understand men's.

That's it – I can't help being who I am, even if it's evil, even if it's just Abdullah forcing me to be this way.

Never mind then, I will reconcile myself to being evil. I'm sure God will understand that I can't help it, that I tried.

I wish I could take my prayer mat and pray to Him, and explain everything, and Say Sorry For What I've Done, what I'm doing, and to Please Rid Me Of The Evil, or if not that, then let me be this way because I can't be otherwise.

I wish I could tell Him how much I'm repulsed by beards that look like pubic hair, and men's bodies that I find plain and artless.

But I've been told it's pointless: He won't listen to me, because I'm *na-paak* – unholy, dirty, and I'm not allowed to pray if I'm living in such a state of sin.

Well, so be it then. Let me embrace evil, and since I'm here now, and have nothing to lose, maybe I should also do all that's prohibited.

…Perhaps I should start by getting a tattoo. I've always wanted one.

Mona Dash

Mona Dash is the author of the novel *Untamed Heart* and two poetry collections, *Dawn-Drops* and *A Certain Way*. She has a Masters in Creative Writing (with distinction) from London Metropolitan University. Mona received a 'Poet of Excellence' award in the House of Lords in 2016. Her work has been published, anthologised and listed in various competitions. Her short story collection *Let Us Look Elsewhere* was shortlisted for the SI Leeds literary awards '18. Her memoir *A Roll of the Dice: a story of loss, love and genetics* has been published recently by Linen Press. Mona is a Telecoms Engineer and MBA, and works in a global technology organisation. Originally from India, she lives in London. www.monadash.net

The Sense of Skin

I watched Ana sleep, her mouth open, the butterfly tattoo on her shoulder poised to fly. Her skin, lavender soap-scented, paper-dry, dolphin-cold. I spooned her and she continued sleeping.

The morning had been busy, with several animals to do. Foxes, rabbits, minks; tool sharpened, inserted into the skin like a needle, taken off like a sock, skin, discarded like clothes. We'd learnt from them, our fathers and uncles who worked on the farm and came home in the evenings, breath like ice, to the crackling fire in the living room. They brought back pelt that was slightly damaged and unfit to be sold, so we always had warm rugs, furs on our mothers' and aunts' shoulders. They brought back cold cuts of rabbit to pickle, or eat with coarse dark rye bread. Here in Ostrobothnia, the scent of skin was always alive.

At home in the evening I filleted the fish, scales collecting on the blade, while Ana watched me, lips parted, teeth uneven like small pebbles. Ana loves animals, she's the kind who walks other peoples' dogs, rehomes straggly cats and lets spiders spin webs in dark corners of the house.

'Do you skin your animals alive?' she asked, her bright green eyes trying to hide her disgust. It wasn't the first time she had questioned, or the first time I'd explained.

'We look after our animals. They die peacefully before we skin. Besides, live animals fight back and can hurt with sharp claws, their fur could get damaged.'

'Over-fed, then slaughtered and skinned. Nice.'

'Have you been talking to the Oikeutta eläimille again?'

'I don't need to talk to animal activists. Don't you think I know? Those Arctic foxes in small cages. You ever seen the fear on their faces?'

'It's not that bad at all.' I was sure she had been talking to someone.

'I went for a walk the other day, over to your cousin's side of the farm. The poor foxes, they don't even howl anymore. Scared to silence. They can smell the scent of dying skin.'

'I can take you for a tour if you want. Please don't walk around like that on your own.' She worried me for an instant, I really needed to be careful about what she saw.

I had met Ana in a bar in the town, a friend's friend introduced us. I liked her from the moment I saw her, so slim, graceful, so different from me. We all got drunk that evening, and I remember sharing numbers. Later she told me I was the exact type she liked. Solid, fit, smiling, and my fingers, she loved my fingers. It'd been three months. I couldn't have enough of her.

But I sensed her restlessness, her doubts, her eyes and mind always asking, searching me. Fur farming was not new to her of course, but she was a teacher and I could see she didn't really like it, unlike other women I knew.

'I will do what I like. Is there nothing else you can do for a living? Your brother moved to Stockholm. He's a lawyer isn't it?'

'Worse. An Accountant.'

She laughed.

We had our dinner outside in the summer evening light, sharing the smorgasbord, Ana chewing the fish delicately, I cutting my steak, watching the blood release. When I skinned I was known to be so skilful that the blood didn't spill. Wine glasses in hand, we watched the night come upon us. I felt like taking her right there but she wanted to put away the plates, brush her teeth, she had such a sense of routine.

I watched her as she slept.

I remembered a night when I lay stroking her arm, the freckles on her paper-skin. She liked that.

'I skinned a seal once, so smooth, so cold. Like you. You won't believe how tight the skin is, stretched firm. When I drew it out, there was a drop of congealed blood, only a globule. And the scent! That sort of flesh, blood-smell…' I said.

She stared at me, got up and left. I thought she was going to the toilet, but she didn't come back for a while. I went to the living area, and found her on the couch, curled like an Arctic fox, a few days old, soft fur waiting to be skinned.

'Coming to bed?'

'I am not sure.'

I sat down next to her. We leaned back on the sofas. I said I wasn't sure why I said that, and she only shrugged. 'You have those animals on your mind always. Helpless skinned animals. Is that how you see me?' I held her, I said it wasn't at all like that. I don't know when I fell asleep. In the morning, she was gone. She had a studio flat in the centre of town, though she spent most nights with me in my cottage on the border of the farm.

What's up? I messaged.

Coming back? I messaged after thirty minutes.

She didn't respond all day. When the moon had climbed half-way up the sky, she came back. We made love like we did whenever she went away and came back; like lost children, like crying animals. Later I said, 'Animal skinning is all I know. There's nothing else I can do.'

'Study. Get a degree. Who skins animals for a living?'

'We do. Fur farmers. Our family has for generations. You can talk to Uncle Vasa and...'

'I just don't like it... wish you could do something different. It's not normal, you know?'

She still didn't get that it was normal for me. Even though my father was no more, and my brother had moved away, I worked on the farm with my cousins. We were used to feeling the ice-air as we skinned one fox after the other, used to taking delight in a perfect skinning. Our farm was renowned for high quality pelt for generations. Ana the teacher. She just thought everyone had to be a person of letters.

We would never know who complained. Ana? Someone else? It was so quick, we had no time to react. The officials were suddenly there, all loud voices and staring eyes, demanding inspection. Norway had banned fur farming a few months ago. The world was now looking at Finland, and searches happened frequently. They found the animals skinned alive, their mouths swinging in horror. Foxes five times their weight in the wild. Our animals were taken away in vans, yelping in fear. They gave us a notice to stop operations. We would be allowed to start only after six months, when the officials checked and certified us a safe practice fur farm. It would take months of effort, years of work, to re-establish ourselves. A hundred years of family tradition, lost.

Ana stood watching, in her red shirt dress. It swung loose around her slim curves.

'You tipped them off, didn't you?'

She didn't react. Her eyes remained cool green.

'You lied. You weren't following procedure.'

'It wasn't us; it was the new apprentices. Cousin Timo hadn't checked.'

'Lies again. You knew.'

'You have ruined everything! Our farm is shut.'

'So much more to do. You could go out there...'

'I will. I will get to this 'out there,' I said.

'Feel guilty at least! This is it, finally your chance of repentance,' she shouted, her words loud in the empty farm. I thought of the skinning, the almost orgasmic delight I felt. Perfection. I would miss it. She left and this time I didn't message her.

Cousin Timo blamed me for bringing Ana to the farm. I retorted it wasn't her, but deep down, I wondered. I shouted he should have been more careful, adopting hasty methods to make more money. We had never fought before; we didn't speak now for days. The days were dull, the farm silent. I needed a break. Then I heard of some friends backpacking to the Far East; Thailand, Cambodia, Bali, India, countries I had seen on maps in school. In spite of what Ana presumed, I would see the world, I would forget her waxy-paper skin, the cold air I had grown up in. I joined them. We travelled away for months, into the tropics, into the heat. I fell into a mass of humanity I didn't know existed. I was in India.

I am on a train from the Mumbai in the west and will go down the coast to Kanyakumari. The others are in Goa, but I'd wanted to see more of this country, to travel all the way to its tips. Everything feels different.

There is a confusing array of options to choose from on the train, 1st A.C. 1st class, 2nd A.C. In order to make my money go far, I ask for a second class sleeper ticket.

'A berth to yourself, but no air-conditioning,' the man at the counter says, his teeth stained from something he is chewing. Later I will learn it is paan; betel nuts wrapped in a leaf, bright red watery juices. I don't want the cold I say. I want my skin to feel, to sweat. I want my skin to feel different from the cold skins I know. The man behind the counter gives that characteristic nod I have been seeing in the country, but can't figure if it's a yes or a no.

'Foreigners prefer air-conditioning,' he says.

'What do they know? I will be fine.'

Indeed, the heat makes my skin sweat. It's not anything I have known. It drips from my armpits and I feel it on my legs, my toes. There is a smell in the air, sweat drying on exposed skin. It envelops me. I wear flip-flops, my pale feet among the many brown feet, dusty like theirs. I observe how their clothes hang loose, folds of which are exposed at times, their legs, skinny, hairy. I am used to the cold, to the silence, to my swift knife spearing warm skin and turning it cold. Here the people surround me and each other. Their eyes smile, even when they try to trick me and charge me extra, or want something from me. They look at me in wonder. They ask to touch my skin; they call me gora. White is a blessing, white is godsend, they say. I am embarrassed.

Inside the train, I have never seen so many human beings in one space, like the minks in a Danish farm I had visited, in cages much smaller than advised. I sit along with six other men on a berth; I like their sweating skin, in shades of brown, light, dark, darker, like the earth outside, like the volcanic soil in the hills of Ostrobothnia. My own skin is paper white in comparison, transparent, unlike theirs, deep like the earth. My body wants to be lost in this crowd.

Every time the train pulls up at a station, people enter in hordes. Once, the man opposite me shoves a few men, 'Out, get out.'

'Hey, what's up?' I ask, surprised.

'They are from general class. No ticket. Shouldn't be here, Sahib.'

'You mustn't call me sahib.' They have explained it is a sign of respect. I don't understand why they feel I deserve any.

They offer me their food – packed boxes of paratha and spicy pickle – even though I say I don't want it. I am being careful. I don't want to fall ill. They show me how to eat with my hands. I wonder what Ana would make of my cut-to-the skin nails now turmeric stained. I suck my fingers. When the train stops at a station, I step out and buy puris served with a watery potato curry, and glasses of sweet brown tea for everyone.

On the second day, one of the men who speaks English gives me some news. There is a 'foreigner woman from England,' and she is walking through the compartments taking pictures of everyone.

'From your country. She will meet you.'

'I am from Finland, not England.' My fellow passengers don't seem to know the difference or care about it.

Two women arrive. The men make space for them, dust the seats. The white girl smiles, holds her hand out, 'Kate.' English, nice, sensible. She is bleached white-blond and I can understand why it is interesting for the Indians. They stare at her and a little girl caresses Kate's hair, as if she is a doll.

The other girl, dark like the dusk; her eyes are the night, her body shines with jewellery. Long danglers on the ears; I count five holes along her ear, each with a different coloured stud. A nose ring. Bangles on her wrists. A long necklace swings on her breast. Anklets on her feet, silver and red. Rings on all her fingers. She wears a loose flowery tunic over baggy trousers. Her feet are wonderfully exposed and there are little rings on her toes. I think of Ana, Ana was bare.

'Pekka.'

'Vaani,' and she holds her hand out now.

I have never seen anything like her. Shining skin smooth seal-like, warm, as if on fire, as if an Aga has been lit behind that skin.

They study together in London. Kate had always wanted to travel in India and Vaani was only too happy to accompany her. Vaani is from southern India, from the very tip.

'That's where you are going to. Kanyakumari.' She explains.

'It's so beautiful here,' Kate says.

I agree. 'Do you like London?' I ask Vaani.

'Yes, of course. And you, you like this?' she moves her slim hands in an arc taking in the compartment, the crowd, the men and their families.

'Yes,' I say even more firmly. For some reason I feel defensive, as if she is mocking them.

'Why are you here? You should be in the first class where Kate and I are. Or at least 2nd A.C,' she continues.

'I like it. What's wrong with it?'

'What's wrong?! Come and visit us and then you will know. It's not like all of India is like this. Dirty, crowded. Squalid.'

'Why have you come to our coach then?'

'Because of Kate, she's the one wanting to take pictures. I am her guide, so that she doesn't get into trouble.' Her lips are full, glossy. Her mouth curves as if she is laughing at us.

Kate is looking out of the window, her camera through the bars.

'Foreigners don't travel in these classes,' Vaani repeats firmly. 'Out of curiosity, what do you do?'

'I am an animal skinner.'

'What? An animal skinner, oh boy.' As if the oh boy isn't incongruous enough, she throws her head back and laughs, louder and louder.

'What's so funny?'

'Do people actually do these kind of things? No wonder you don't care what class you travel on.'

'Fur farming is our family profession. There's nothing to laugh about.'

'Tradition. How cute.'

Kate wants to photograph the compartment; the set of smiling men, the family with the two little girls, me, Vaani opposite me. We smile and hold our fingers up in V signs.

I talk to them. I find myself describing the sunset over the farm, how the sky changes colour, pink, blue, then lights up orange and red for an hour or more until the sun sets. How everything is so quiet when I wake up, the morning air so fresh, when I walk on the grass, the ice crunching beneath my shoes. I walk to the cages and lead the animals out. They know me, they trust me. My hands are magic; I can soothe skin. 'I don't hurt the animals, I am gentle,' I say, 'even when I skin them. I am so gentle.' They listen to me in rapt attention. I notice Vaani rests her hand on my arm, she isn't laughing anymore.

'Why don't you join us for a drink? Vaani says. Outside, the sun has moved almost the entire span of the sky and I wait for it to sink suddenly like it does here, unlike the prolonged sunsets in Finland. I follow them. People, so many people, sitting on haunches, standing on their toes, along the length of the train. Then suddenly things are posher and everything seems cleaned in a car wash. It's very private, their cabin has a door which can be locked. Safe for women, they tell me. The air is fresh and cool. Though it's not as cold, it reminds me of my skinning room.

Kate has some beer in her suitcase, Vaani pulls out a small bottle of Jack Daniel. They giggle as they pour it into metal water bottles.

'So that no one knows what we are drinking if they come to check! We aren't meant to drink publicly, railway rules!'

'Oh I didn't know you couldn't drink on a train... and well, I didn't know Indian girls drink.'

'What do you know!' she laughs.

We sit next to each other. We talk. I have lived long in cold, clean rooms. This stickiness, the warmth on my skin, I like it, do you understand why? I search Vaani's eyes for an answer.

'Intriguing. So different,' she says finally. I can see she is curious, I reach out and let my fingers run on her arm. She laughs and Kate rolls her eyes.

It is past midnight. We have eaten food from the pantry. The drinks are over. 'Time for bed,' Kate yawns. She plugs in her headphones, puts on an eye mask. She has the lower berth and Vaani hoists herself on the top berth.

'Come,' she says, patting the space next to her. I point at Kate, 'what about her?'

'She sleeps like a babe. Also she won't mind. She knows me!'

I climb up and sit, legs folded, head bent. She switches the main lights off, and flicks a reading light.

I look at her, her eyes, her skin, mostly her skin. She removes her top, then the rest.

'You smell good,' I whisper.

'Indian jasmine, don't you know?' She has tattoos, small shapes on her arms, shoulders. I see a seal, glowing black on her left thigh. Unashamedly warm. The berth isn't long enough for me, and she laughs that I have to keep my legs bent. She lies flat on me. We learn to inhabit the small space, to make the best of it. Am I hurting her? She smiles no. And when I inspect her, as I do my animals, every crevice, every fold, she doesn't judge me, she doesn't call me animal skinner, instead she laughs, she spreads, she arches, she turns around. Open, trusting.

All night, her laughing whispers, her scented skin with unfamiliar smells, all night our connected bodies fall in with the train's gentle trembling. I am meant to go back to Finland, Cousin Timo has said the farm will resume soon. But I find myself agreeing with Vaani, yes, I will visit her in Kanyakumari, yes I will stay longer.

I like her skin.

I let the sweat drown our skin.

Jason Deelchand

Jason Deelchand has previously been shortlisted for the Guardian/4th Estate Short Story Prize. He has taught English at secondary schools in Bath, Cornwall, Bristol, and Shanghai. He was born in Epsom to an English mother and a Mauritian father. His heroes are Malcolm X and Roberto Bolaño.

All for Love

Tonight, gentleman, we celebrate the two-hundredth anniversary of the formation of our society, and I have been invited to speak about one of our great founders: the honourable Reverend Winter.

[Applause in the golden hall.

Paintings line the wall. The applause dies

to a single cough.]

Thank you. Reverend Winter was one of the finest men in the history of our fine and faithful ward of Prosperity. His father amassed a considerable fortune as a merchant, and Reverend Winter was raised to be a humble and God-fearing fellow. He studied at Jesus College, Cambridge, though as we know he left that unseemly place to found – alongside other great men – the ward of Prosperity upon this great hill.

His academic excellence cannot be challenged, though some have tried. He was a man that knew the Word of our Lord with such depth and recall that if one were to see him on one of his habitual strolls around our shining ward, one could call out to him a Biblical reference and he would instantly retrieve the exact scripture from the powerful maze of his mind.

– Reverend Winter! (one might say) – how about Job 5:4?

And he'd reply:

His children are far from safety, and they are crushed in the gate,
Neither is there any to deliver them.

He was a stern man, we know that to be true, but his sternness served his flock well. He was a wonderful speaker – such a wonderful speaker. On Sunday mornings, the faithful men (and their wives and children) of our noble Prosperity would gather to hear him deliver the Word of our Lord with his signature style and bombast. His sermons were so powerful, so persuasive, that men even came from neighbouring parishes to hear him speak. An attendance-limit had to be introduced, and some neighbouring parishes even had to have their services abolished!

[A brief drizzle
of laughter and chuckling.
Webs upon the beams.]

Reverend Winter's most powerful sermons were delivered on the somewhat sensitive topic of what we may refer to as "the Trade," and what he referred to as "the God-ordained traffic of those inferior races and brutes" whom were brought to the ports of the city beneath us and transported across the Atlantic. At the time, there was an increasing discontent regarding the Trade. Simple-minded liberals were arguing that the Trade was a cruel practice, that the inferior peoples suffered, and that it was against God's Will. Reverend Winter, a mighty apologist for the Trade, demolished the liberal arguments from his pulpit. He deployed his most fearsome weapons: the booming voice, those swelling pauses, his simple phrasing that spoke to the common men of the city; and of course, he used the Word of our Lord. I have some samples from his sermons. Please forgive my delivery:

"We are rescuing the heathens. We are bringing them to the light of our Lord from their wheezing and filthy state of brutality. If you ask me, people, what we are doing is an act of love. Act... of... love."

And another:

"The prosperity of the nation, and our Prosperity – our fine ward, you see – all depends upon subjugating inferior races. What would you prefer: that we enlist our own countrymen and women to toil in the colonies? Jobs for the ordinary man are already being taken by the Welsh and the Irish; very soon we'll have the damn frogs hopping over here and seducing our women – OUR women! Look at cities across the land: decent, hard-working Englishmen are struggling to increase their yields. Every other European kingdom worth their salt is wise enough to increase their capital in distant lands: should we fall beneath them? The... trade... is... great."

And one other example from those fiery years:

"We are told clearly, people, *'slaves, submit to your masters'* – what more evidence is needed? The Word is absolute truth, is it not? Am I not correct, people? God has ordered us to subjugate the lesser peoples of the Earth to serve us as we serve Him. We... serve... him."

[Applause and encouragements.

Bloody good reading, chap!

Red cheeks and thin grins.]

Thank you, Jacob – you're too kind. Please... thank you. I'm sure you can imagine that the fine people that heard his words were thumping their feet, their eyes bulging with satisfaction!

The thirst for his words and wisdom was such that he trained one of his servants to scribe for him, and he had his thoughts written onto small pieces of paper which were collected into baskets and taken to Prosperity Abbey where they were unloaded from the tower so that the papers scattered throughout the streets like leaves; he had the same done at the Abbey in the city. In this way, the common folk were able to learn from him each day. There are too many of these wonderful snippets to go through, but I've picked my favourite three:

"Simple-minded liberals oppose the trade. Sad. They clearly do not care about the country. Do you?"

"Lots of mindless talk at this present time. Academics (or is it academTRICKS?) are spreading lies as usual. And people wonder why ordinary citizens are starving? If we don't enslave inferior races then they will steal your jobs."

"Lots of immigrants stealing jobs. What next, our women? OUR women? Many of them eat children. A plague of locusts. Liberals and academTRICKS ruining this great nation."

Opposition to the Trade grew, but so too did our forefathers' estates. Reverend Winter, alongside our most esteemed founders, created banking institutions and great corporations from which their harvests increased.

I realise my time is short this evening, chaps, so I'll quicken the pace. The years passed. A demon-induced man by the name of Thomas Clarkson wrote a series of spluttering, lie-riddled polemics. One of these was titled: 'Is it right to enslave men against their will?' Most right-minded men could answer this immediately, but a greater number of liberal fools were poking their heads above the ground like a bunch of short-sighted and dim-witted moles. Thankfully, Reverend Winter rained God-ordained fury upon them. It was to be his last sermon. I will read an abridged version:

"Must we regress, people, into our animalistic, brutalistic, inferioristic, state-of-being? We, the fine men of Prosperity, have brought untold wealth to this nation, to this land of England; and how are we repaid and regarded? I tell you: we are reprimanded and defamed! Reprimanded... and... defamed. Our great names and this great nation – and it is a great nation, people, the greatest nation on Earth, am I not correct? Our great nation is being abused by these simple-minded liberals and academtricks. You know why I call them that? They appear to be academic, but they are full of tricks, see? People love it when I say that: academtricks. Clever, yes? Anyway, this is a debasement that – I'm sure you will agree, people – that our Lord God shall not stand for. This – what is his name? Darkson? Doubting Thomas Darkson? I call him that, you see? This Darkson fellow would have us become slaves. He wants us to become slaves to European nations, and perhaps even further afield. Remember Saint-Domingue? I shudder at the thought. Mindless Thomas Darkson. What... a... buffoon. You laugh? Yes, laugh with me. Say it with me: what a buffoon!

Our strong, righteous men, our sailors in our ports – how do you think they feel about all this? I tell you, if I were a sailor and I saw this Clarkson fellow... I don't have to say any more. I don't want the academtricks or simple-minded liberals to have any ammunition. But I tell you about this Darkson, Clarkson, Sharkson fellow: I wouldn't advise him to walk the streets of our city, or out in Liverpool, for example. Do you follow me?

This Clarkson buffoon asks: is it right to enslave men against their will? Can you believe that? I think I know the answer. Do you know the answer, people? Say it with me now: YES! Yes, it is. It is right to enslave a man against their will, because a man's will is not always in accordance with God's Will, and that is the only Will that has any authority. And this Will – His Will, you follow – His Will is ordained to us – you and I, that is, the rich men of this nation – and if we believe that it is His Will to enslave men, then enslave them we shall – women and children, too. It is our moral right, our moral imperative, our moral duty. A... moral... absolute. This is all for love, people. All... for... love."

[Thunderous applause.

Within it, there is laughter and

an appreciation of the reach of tentacles.]

Thank you. Please... thank you. As we all know, gentlemen, this was to be Reverend Winter's last sermon. His flock of mighty merchants and financiers (as well as their women and children) likely all felt a renewed sense of peace, the kind that comes after hearing the Word of our Lord. I can hear their affirmations now:

- Hear! Hear!

- Splendid!

- Truth be told, Reverend!

- Glory to Him, our Father in heaven!

And so on. On that April morning a heavy snow had fallen; a clear sign from our Lord: our forefathers were justified. Reverend Winter went for his habitual Sunday afternoon stroll to Wulfstan Woods. When he did not return at his habitual time of six o'clock, his agitated servant called upon his neighbours. Those fine fellows of Prosperity – our forefathers – gathered their horses and their hounds and went to Wulfstan Woods in search of Reverend Winter. Not one of those men, not hound nor horse, ever returned, and no trace of them was ever found.

We are their fruits, chaps. All these years later we continue to strive, and to build upon each generations' harvests. Some ask: what became of them? Is it all legend? Is it simply some myth to explain our prosperity and Our Prosperity?

We believe, chaps – we know, rather – that our Lord brought them to Him, that they ascended to heaven like Elijah, a recognition of their strength, their unshakeable faith against the hurricane of a flawed social movement opposed to their faithful acts. These movements exist today, gentlemen. They rise to attack our shores like unfaithful ocean waves. There are barbarian hordes at our walls! And we have such an idle and indolent workforce. We must act in order to prosper! We must keep our particular organisation, and the societies that we are in connection with, close and well-oiled. I ask that the Lord continues to provide us with the strength and the wisdom to maintain and increase Our Prosperity.

To finish, I would like to remind us all, gentlemen, of our rite of passage, when each of us spent a night in Wulfstan Woods on our eighteenth and twenty-first birthdays to mark our respects in honour of those fine fellows who laid the foundations for our prestige and power. I tell you this: in those dark woods many one of us has heard the fast gallop of hooves (angels on horses, of course), as well as angered barks (Cerberus reprimanded, no doubt); still others have seen flames (of the Lord, surely), appearing through the thickets; whilst every single one of us has heard the creaking of branches and moans and sighs, the echoes of angels mourning the sacrifice of Reverend Winter and our fine forefathers. Each year we remember them and praise them, and Prosperity still prospers to this day.

[All stand and all applause.

What comes next?

They continue to decide.]

Lisun: I'ma speak your tongue 'cause my original tongue been torn out an' discarded. I'll speak yours, then, 'cause mostly you seem only to hear y'own tongue. I'ma speak tru', too, even though you don't seem to pay much 'tention to the tru'. He 'ave his chance to speak. Is you gonna' lisun t' my word? My voice second, innit? Some voice start thing; some voice end – echoes in the Chasm.

See 'im: the sinnerman walkin' on them cobbled street, blowin' into 'im 'ands, cold, red-faced. Y' know 'bout the hidden things beneath them streets, yeah? The tappin', groans an' that? Do you know 'bout the bones under the foundations of them stately 'omes? Do you know 'bout the circlin' paths, those thirstin' in the dark?

Seed of discord been sown. His diabolic rhetoric twists, hangin' in the air, clinging to 'im army. That's how words is, innit? They cling, grip, infest, burrow, seep, cloud. Other words be coolin', soothin' like a balm. All depend on the speaker.

See 'im: the sinnerman walkin' 'long a frozen dirt path. He go to them woods. Y'eard of Wulfstan Woods? Nah, didn't think so. Snow cover all. The sun left quick. Was it God that done it? Did he make the night swoop down? The sinnerman din't think 'bout it. He have a sickness in him mind. He should'a turn back, but he too proud. He struggle in the snow. He trip of'en. He grab at the trunk of bare trees. Him hands tingle and itch. Serrated nails glide 'cross his skin. No noise or echo or song in those woods, only his sinkin' steps in that impossible snow. No light above him; no light in the distance. Them woods was plucked from – how we call it? linear, yeah – from linear paths and times, placed on some level terrain.

Do you understand, sir or ma'am? Ha. I don't reckon. Why is it some people can't unnerstan'? Is it that they got minds but refuse to think?

Lisun some more, then. A moan rise to his red ears. He stop, look above. Something creaking in the wind. A frozen rope, noosed, hangin' from a snapped branch. The sinnerman frowns and scoffs. He lean up 'gainst a tree trunk which is scarred with deep slashes. The sinnerman scoffs and smiles.

Horses galloping in the distance, faces a' clouded with steam. The rocking of a ship on sullen waves; a bell clangin'. The sinnerman feel the ground beneath him tilt one way then the nex'. He frowns and mumbles.

See him, then: he's lost, tryin' to retrace his steps but findin' only the blank snow and the same trees and distances. A warm breeze caresses his face and he can smell sugar-cane fields, flowers, and violet delights. In his shoes there is sand and dirt and barb'd wire. He fall to floor, clutchin' his feet. He smell urine and shit; it cover 'im, but it ain't his own. He shouts. He bares his teeth to the endless expanse. Another frozen rope on a snapped branch above. His heart thump, thump, thump. He begins to wheeze. Hear him.

Now lisun elsewhere: in the fog of what's called Prosperity, a servant is callin'. She run 'long them cobbled streets and knock at the neighbour's door. She frightened; she excited. Can you see her? Do you see any of what I'm sayin'? What about beneath them streets? See that? I think some peoples can't see. Why's that? Maybe some people likes to avert their eyes from the things that convict them. Maybe they don't like to see things which contradict their comforts.

See this, then: riders on horseback goin' in search of their voice and their shield, movin' slow across snow-covered fields. When they at the edge of the Wulfstan Woods their horses and hounds pause, refusing to enter. And what nex'? The horses and hounds is whipped and beaten because these type of men think that violence leads to submission. But them horses and hounds remain still. Those twenty men snarl. They stumble into the woods. They hold torches in their hands; they hide a rotting in their hearts. How 'bout you? Ha. Don't mind me, as the sayin' goes – don't mind me, sir or ma'am.

See this: in the midst of the woods their torches are muted. All around them they can hear the tapping of chains which rises and fades with each one of their frowns. One of them shout: Jesus! He sees a frozen rope. It's noosed, hangin' from a tree. One of them feel a burning on his forehead; he scream out, agonised. They all go to him to see that his forehead been seared with a cross. He thumps his head into the snow, sobbing.

Then come gun-shots and snapping at the trees and at the earth around them so they scamper in retreat and huddle 'gainst one another as arrows sweep into the snow beside them and they shriek – shriek, shriek, shriek. Howling of human-beings in the shadows around them. A faded torch reignites and the man holdin' it sees a face in the darkness which is covered in white ash and has blood leaking from the eyes. They decide to leave the woods and return to the daylight.

But they ain't getting away, is they? Feel, sir or ma'am, feel their shivers and their fright. Watch them as they plod through the snow. Gather round, if you like. Get a sense of them feeling a tightness in they chests, a chafing of their collars 'gainst the thin skin of they necks which thump, thump, thump. Two fellows fall to the floor, a great weight 'pon their chests. Their lungs fill with needles; they got no air to call out. They ignored, too, which ain't a nice feelin'.

Some others feel a burning rise in their throats. They lift up – puppets with their heads suspended, held by something wailing above. A few attempt to fall to their knees but they hang limp, midway to the ground. They gargle 'gainst a pressure which cracks their tracheas and snaps their necks.

Lisun.

Feel.

Do you feel it, too? Some will, I reckon. But most peoples refuse to feel, innit? They numb to the roots of Humanity. Also, one thing I know is this: feelings is complex, and people struggle with complex things.

What about this, then? Let's see what you make of this. Others of them was pushed to the ground, held down, then entered. Yep. They was entered, crying into the snow. Horrific, innit? They cry into the snow, but the snow ain't cold or wet, like, it's dry and rough, wooden and rusting. Sawdust fills their throats, covers their eyes. They scream, coughing shards of bark. Abused. Pain burns through them.

And yet we are the abused and the pain of centuries lives within us. Did you know that? Horrific, innit? Anyway, they stop screaming when wings wrap 'round their necks; instead, they squeal.

Lisun: not long now, like. The remaining men – the mighty men (is that what the other fella said?) of that mighty place which was built on the backs of stolen human-beings – all those remaining men was blue in the face. They wheezed. Their eyes was bulging, thumping, near to bursting. They was wheezin' their last air: lisun. They rise from the ground and hang in the air: see them? All of them hanging in the air, wheezin'. All their necks is cracked and twisted, all them moan in those stilled woods. That woods is full of their wheezin' forever – always, lisun. But that ain't enough, man; that ain't enough, woman; that ain't enough young children, nephews and nieces, cousins and aunties and uncles, brothers and sisters, fathers and mothers and orphans and the neglected and the adopted. There needs to be more than just wheezin'.

They still there, like. Still wheezin' – hear them? I'm not sure you do. What about beneath them cobbled streets? Remember when I said about them? Or is it only us – the great Us, the scattered, the once destitute diaspora that rebuild one step at a time – is it only us that can unner'stan?

Nah. I reckon everyone can. We all human-beings, innit? We all experienced sparks of this, sensations of this. Our whole history been like this. It's everywhere. It's above them streets, now. I hear their voices to this day. Not the loud voices that you speak, or those voices which dominates the land, but the voices of those lowly-bent heads and them hunched-walkers who have poisons spat into their mouths by those loud and polished voices. I hear the voices of those who ain't even got tongues, and those who speak despite the shackles 'round their mouths.

But why some peoples refuse to lisun, then? They got ears, but they can't hear! Maybe they minds is so full of shit that they ears become clogged. Maybe. Maybe you'll lisun, ey?

Flic Everett

Flic Everett is a food magazine editor (*Vegan Living*) and freelance journalist. She has written several non-fiction books, and has been a feature writer and columnist for 25 years for UK newspapers and magazines. Her true love is fiction – she self-published a novel in 2012, and is now writing another. Unfortunately, reading other peoples' novels and Twitter get in the way. She lives in the West Highlands, with her partner Andy, a spaniel and an elderly cat, and likes long walks, cooking, and reading thrillers in the bath. She has one grown-up son, and her ambition is to write fiction for a living and run a pygmy goat sanctuary.

The End of the Neighbourhood

I don't want to go into space, but my mum says I have to. We all do – all the people that won the lottery for places. She was so relieved when the news arrived, she cried. Then she wiped her face, leaving streaks of watery black across her cheeks, and said, "so, we're saved."

I didn't feel saved. It seemed like another death to me, the unknowable darkness out there, and the promise of rescue, so far away it may as well not exist at all. It's like when they talked about heaven in the old days, living your life on the basis that it was all going to be alright one day, if you just went to church and paid your bills, and didn't do anything adulterous or murderous. Then it would all have been worth it, because you got a golden cloak and wings and harps, and could spend eternity looking down on everyone else, judging them.

I didn't want to judge anyone, I just wanted to stay here, on earth, seeing Maya at school every day and going past Mr McLeod's house every afternoon on my way home, checking he was ok because the curtains had been opened.

"What if they're open from the day before and he died in the night?"

Maya asked me once. I hadn't thought of it, and I briefly felt worried. I'd have to go out in the evening and look to see if he'd closed them. I did that a few times, but then life overtook me – something I needed to watch, or homework, or my mum needing help with the food, and I left him to his own devices. Mr McLeod isn't coming into space with us.

I went to see him, after the lottery, and he made me a cup of tea with two sugars, and said, "I've had my life."

"But you'll die if you stay," I said. He said, "we're all going to die, I've made my peace with it," and then we talked about his daughter, Alice, who lives thousands of miles away. "She won a place, but she's not going," he said. "Her husband didn't get one so she'd rather stay."

My mum behaved as though everyone on earth must be desperate to win, she hadn't slept for weeks, waiting to find out. I'd come downstairs in the morning to get ready for school, and she would be sitting with her hot water, staring out of the window at the empty garden, and the pavement beyond, where the neighbourhood cats liked to lie in the shade of the cars.

"Why are you up so early?" I asked, and she said "I can't sleep till I know if we're going to survive."

I was too young to be scared of death. I couldn't imagine it – maybe nobody can. The headlines were full of extinction and animals and birds we'd never see again, but I thought it was odd that we'd happily eaten them all or ignored them till recently – so what did it matter whether they were eaten by us, or killed by sun and floods and storms? My mum had always hated insects but now, suddenly, the lack of them was a tragedy. There was no more batting uselessly round the kitchen after flies in summer, no spiders that made her scream, haring randomly across the carpet. I only noticed the lack of humming – there were no flowers left, and all the bees had gone. They were supposed to be taking some kind of hives with us and breeding bees for the new place, and I couldn't think how that was going to work on the shuttles. But my mum was insistent that they had it all organised.

It was a week till we were meant to go, and she was in a constant state of stress about what to take – each of us was only allowed one small bag, like when we took a cheap flight once, and had our scuffed plastic cases measured by a box at the check-in desk. They had just fitted and my mum said, "thank god for that," but she seemed angry.

We couldn't take Cookie, either. Our dog was old and tired, and Mr McLeod was going to look after him for us.

I wanted to feel terrible about that, but I knew how much easier it would be for Cookie to take his usual slow walks and lie on somebody's feet in a place he understood. The air in the new place was meant to be fine now, but mum didn't want to risk it, not knowing whether a dog's lungs could handle it.

"You can't take that," she said to me, lifting my prizewinning cup out of my hands. I was trying to choose which clothes I'd need – it would be air conditioned, so "it may be a bit chilly" said the article Mum had read to me. "Take clothing suitable for a bright Autumn day."

That made no sense – for years, every season had been the same, blazing hot, and sometimes a pinkish smog fell down like a curtain over the cars and houses, and it was hard to breathe. A couple of kids I half-knew had died during the last one, and Mum had made me stay in with the curtains drawn and the window frames stuffed with wet cloths till it lifted a few weeks later.

It was hard to remember bright Autumn days, so I just stuffed some light sweaters and a couple of T shirts in, and an old book my dad had given me, Three Men in a Boat. "It's the funniest book ever written," he said. "One day, you'll laugh till you cry." I hadn't yet opened it, but it had lasted longer than him, so I thought I should take it.

"Why can't I take the cup?" I asked. It was the only thing I'd ever won.

"Because there'll be nowhere to put it," said my Mum. "When we get there, we're all living in the blocks, till they establish proper zones. You know that."

I did, but I hadn't really paid attention. "What blocks?" I said, and she didn't like my tone.

"The ones we'll live in, with everyone else who got lucky," she said, as if she was biting the heads off flowers and spitting them out. She had liked gardening, in the old days. "The ones that are saving our bloody lives."

I shrugged and she left the room, snapping the door behind her. "And hurry up with that bag," she called from the hall. "We need to sort the car out and leave room for food."

It was a two-day drive to the shuttle and she had been worrying about traffic jams, even though nobody was leaving 'until everyone is accounted for,' as the ads kept saying. "Everyone who won," I said to myself, whenever they came on. And our rations were so low now, I was pretty sure she could fit them in her purse with room to spare. The water tub was a problem, it needed two of us to lift it, and nobody seemed sure how much the shuttles were taking "just until we get irrigation sorted out." I assumed they would have it organised when the time came.

Two days before we were leaving, Maya came over after school. Knowing this was the last time felt so momentous, we didn't know what to say to each other. We sat at opposite ends of my bed, snorting at the absurdity of the situation, and scrolling through our phones to see who else we'd ever met was going and staying. "Steve Willis!" She said. "Good luck with that."

"He won't even be in the same zone," I said, and she said, "Oooh, zone, listen to you," and poked my foot.

"Are you scared?" I asked, after a silence.

"I don't know," she said. "I can't really imagine it. Are you?"

"Yeah, a bit," I told her. Every time I thought about the darkness, and leaving everyone and everything I'd ever known, to go and live in some kind of oxygenated commune, I wanted to laugh hysterically. What would I message her about then? "We have irrigated the space-carrots and they are growing well. Are you dead yet?"

The fear had been sitting in the pit of me for months, ever since my mum opened the email, and looked up, her eyes glowing.

I didn't want to say that though – what use would it be? When Maya left, we hugged, and promised to keep in touch, and agreed that one day, maybe there'd be another mass leaving, and I'd see her up there.

Or things would change, and I'd come back down. We'd be adults by then, but maybe we'd still like each other. "Good luck," she said, standing in the doorway. "Good luck to you too," I said and hugged her. She was stiff and embarrassed in my arms and I let her go and laughed it off as if I'd been melodramatic deliberately.

The day before we left, the car was packed, and the house was cleaned – I didn't see the point, it would belong to the government after this, and I thought they could clean it themselves. Mum said, "I don't want to leave a mess behind." I didn't comment on the irony of that, considering the looming mess we were planning to avoid.

She asked me if I'd take Cookie over to Mr McLeod's, because she didn't want to cry when she said goodbye to him. So I clipped his lead on, and walked across, with his cushion and bowl clamped uncomfortably under my arm. He was too old for toys now.

Mr McLeod opened the door without saying anything, and I walked in. I sat down at his old kitchen table, as usual, and started to explain Cookie's feeding regime and how many biscuits he was allowed, then I realised Mr McLeod wasn't saying anything. His eyes were wet, and he was rubbing Cookie's head without really seeing him.

"I'll miss you, you know," he said eventually. "You and your Mum."

I nodded. I'd never seen an adult I wasn't related to cry before.

"We'll miss you too," I said.

"Are you looking forward to it?" He asked me, sitting down on one of his blue kitchen chairs. I must have seen those chairs a thousand times. My whole life, I'd just known that Mr McLeod had blue kitchen chairs and assumed I'd be sitting in them forever. Like I knew Maya was my friend, and that this was where we lived. A ball of something fiery was in my chest, making its way up to my throat, some kind of noise was going to come out, so I shut my eyes and breathed until it was forced back down.

"I guess not," said Mr McLeod. He offered me a biscuit – he made them himself, once a month, from his saved rations – and I took one. He had one too, and we sat in silence, eating together, watching Cookie sniffing round the kitchen.

When I got home, I messaged Maya, "will you look after my prize cup till I get back?" and she messaged, "yeah, if I can tell people it's mine."

I sent her a thumbs up.

There was another smog the next morning, and my mum was watching the news when I got up, crouched forward on the sofa the way she drove, alert to danger and setbacks.

"It's going to take longer than I thought," she said, over her shoulder.

"We should go in a minute."

I looked for Cookie, because she needed to jump into the back of the car, then I remembered she wasn't ours any more. She was at her friend's house, probably thinking we'd be coming back soon, like we usually did.

"I know it's tough," said my mum. "I'll just have a wash, and then we'll go. And on the journey, we'll try and think of all the good things about what we're doing, and how lucky we are to have this chance."

I nodded. I heard her footsteps on the stairs, and the bathroom door click shut. Without thinking any further than the next second, I let myself out of our front door. I told myself I was going to see Cookie, to say one last goodbye, but I kept on walking past Mr McLeod's house, where the curtains were still drawn, past the turn-off to Maya's road where she'd be starting to get ready for school, and I carried on. Getting through the smog was like walking through the tropical house at the zoo, where my dad used to take me. But with a hood over your face, and a fine layer of gritty particles that clung to any exposed skin. I kept walking, though I couldn't see where I was going. I heard the news blasting from a parked car – 'Leavers are arriving at the site, and have been coming since yesterday. Boarding commences in two days' time, though there are concerns…' the voice muffled and vanished back into the smog. In the distance I heard my mother's frightened shout. I kept walking. She would go without me. Or she wouldn't. I thought about Mr McLeod's blue chairs and how I would sit in them again and eat biscuits and Cookie would be there, heaving one of her huge sighs, as if all the air was leaving her body at once. I'd message Maya later, and tell her I hadn't gone.

"Keep the cup anyway," I'd say. I smiled at the thought of it, and walked on, into the hot blanket of cloud where I lived.

Marie-Gabrielle Gallard

Marie-Gabrielle Gallard was born in France, and also lived in Germany and Belgium as a child. She moved to the UK to study at Newcastle University and graduated in July 2019 with a First Class Honours Degree in English Literature with Creative Writing. She started writing prose in her native language, French, when she was ten years old, before switching to English at fifteen. Now twenty-one, she wishes to remain in the world of literature, to keep reading and writing, and continue postgraduate studies in the field.

black cross

a nd I remember, my small hand holding onto my smaller pen, marking my skin with a black cross. On that day, to remind myself to ask mom or dad to sign the authorization. On another day, to remind myself to pack my toothbrush with my pajamas. Staining the back of my hand until I'd remember, and the dark ink would only smear and smudge once I'd remembered, washed away by soap and water. But on this hand, this older hand of mine, one black cross hasn't been rinsed away. The tap has quenched rather than drenched. And like a seed under the rain, it has grown, rising a tree of crosses on my hand, spreading branches on my forearm and scattering leaves on my arm. The faded petals of forgotten memories that haven't bloomed and blown away find themselves in each of the twenty-three black crosses scarring my skin. Never to be scrubbed or scoured away, tattooed from the beginning of my hand to the end of my arm are recollections that I can't recall;

medical records. Name: Doe. First Name: Jane. Gender: Female. Address: Unknown. Date of Birth: Unknown. Observations: Brain of the patient displays injuries to the hippocampus and to the diencephalon thalamus. Patient also demonstrating recurrent epileptic seizures. Episodes followed by memory losses, exhibited by severe retrograde amnesia and degrees of anterograde amnesia. Procedural memory relatively intact. Patient presently maintains the ability to acquire and apply new knowledge, also able to carry a conversation coherently. Serious deficiencies in declarative memory. Patient unable to remember any event prior to admission to hospital, unaware of present location and date, past childhood and early adulthood entirely forgotten, as well as personal identity forgotten. Diagnosis: Amnestic Syndrome;

there are one hundred and seven tattoo shops in New York, at least there are one hundred and seven listed on the Yellow Pages. I don't hesitate before the shop windows, I push the door open and I walk in. Bells fail to be heard over whichever metal, rock, pop or indie music blaring from the speakers. The tattooist though never fails to hear me come in, always speaking first. And I know this is not it. I turn around, I pull open the door and I walk out. Leaning against a streetlamp, I cross out the name and the address of the forty-second tattoo shop from the torn paper. I stare at the forty-third, mapping the city and locating the shop in my mind, tracing my way to it. And again, I push the door open and I walk in. The tattoo parlor is empty but for a slender man crouching on the countertop by the windows. His long legs are bent in front of him, balancing his feet between the solid surface behind and the empty space before him. He looks up from his phone, he glances at me, he looks down to his phone. I stop in my tracks. He doesn't speak first. I speak first. I ask him if he knows the tattoos on my arm. "I do." I also ask him if he knows the girl with the tattoos on my arm. "I do." I wonder if he can give me any information about her. He stays on his phone, ignoring me and my question. If not her name, I ask for his name. He laughs without laughter. "My name? My name's Ash. What's your name this time?" I look down. I catch the sight of my hospital wristband around my wrist. "Doe." His head snaps up. "What?" I repeat myself. "It's Doe. Jane Doe." He stares at me and step by step he starts to slowly lose his footing. His feet tip, his ankles turn, his legs and his pelvis and his torso tilt downwards, as his body dips and drops towards the void before him. He's falling and he's falling further. Before he tears his eyes away from my eyes, and he's leapt and landed steadily on his two feet. He starts for the door and speaks up, his back to me. "You want to know about her? I'll show you.";

04/21 i was wrong. i didn't need to know. i certainly didn't need to do any of this shit. stalking strangers, tracking junkies, digging arm deep in bags of trash. for this. i should've stayed there, in those smelling clothes, on that stinking mattress. counting flies. maybe if i hadn't moved for one minute, just one minute more, i might've convinced myself i was dead. might've even convinced the police when they'd have showed up not minutes later, but months later. though they wouldn't have needed much convincing from me. there'd been enough left behind. empty bottles, belts with needles, rusty hangers, shiny knives, they choose. or i could've made myself stop from moving for more than minutes. and this time, i'd have chosen – "You're not done. Not until I say you are. Not until you see it, all of it." Ash rips the notebook from my hands, tears through the pages and tosses it back to me, open to the last entry. He doesn't wait for me to read, or for me to even look down to read. He's already at the other end of the room, turning upside down the table, and the bedside table, and the bed, throwing incriminations back at me, words and sentences of hers, images of hers, marks of hers, anything that belonged to her. He's pacing back and forth in the small studio too small for him, and he's mumbling, he's rambling, he's raving. He shouts. He shouts at her. Her name was Gold because she said that she had the memory of a goldfish. I find remnants of her name in the color of her nail polish and her eyeshadow and her eyeliner by the sink. I also find her name in the color of her hair, at least in the remaining locks of her hair. The last yellowish strands of the dye are slowly shampooed and showered away from my head now. But the bleach still blemishes my hair, remembering the blond woman before me, like everything around me remembers all of the dark and light-haired women before me. The notebooks reading personal thoughts as well as impersonal names, addresses and phone numbers, the newspaper articles carefully cut or casually torn, the flying pages of small Post-it Notes and the large missing posters, the pictures spread on the wall or scattered on the floor. There's a woman on all those images, sometimes it's a posed photo, sometimes a snapshot, sometimes a sketch. There's the same woman always caught with a different number of black crosses on her arm. Ash turns and stills, "She searched for them. She wanted to know who she was before, find a reason why they'd all been forgotten, why *she'd* been forgotten, abandoned and dumped to wake up in a deserted crack house. Gold was angry. Gold was *nothing* but angry. What are you? What are you doing this for?" There are thirteen crosses on one picture, four on another, eleven on another one. "I don't know. I guess because of the crosses." He stares silently at me and doesn't answer. I look down at the diary on the floor. *04/27 i don't want to remember anymore. i want to forget. let me forget. please let me forget. i can't remember. stop. just stop remembering;*

good morning/afternoon/evening, I am sorry to bother you at such a time of the day/night, but I couldn't come before. I do believe that you have met [insert name of relevant Jane Doe], and that you were [insert relationship with relevant Jane Doe]. I would like to apologize for the pain that she might've caused you and I would like to explain [...]. I carry the crumpled paper of jumbled words clumsily jotted down everywhere we go. Cruising in his car through the deserts' routes and the coasts' highways, his arm hangs out the window while both of my hands fold protectively around my introductory note on my lap. Crossing little towns and big cities, crashing in cheap motels, escaping in the cheap motels' toilets, my starting sentences are always nestled between my palms. I read and I proofread my words, I learn them, I practice them and I act them. Until I don't need the paper to remember them anymore. Or until I stand alone in front of a closed door, and the echo of the bell fades, and the bark of the dog approaches, and I can't remind myself of the words anymore, and I fumble in my pocket because I need the paper to remember. I don't often find myself finishing the first sentence, sometimes I don't get the first word out, sometimes the first syllable, before I am jumped on, screamed at, shouted at, or before the door is slammed back to my face. And I hear it all. A sighed Gold. A startled Bonnie. A smiled Amaryllis. A frowned Heather. A tired Camille. An exhausted Cammie. An angry September. A whispered Phoebe. Just a gasp, someone inhaling or exhaling sharply. Or just a meow. Or just a woof. And by then the written words don't matter anymore, their spoken sentences mean more. They start telling me stories about the Jane Doe they've met. There's one about how she called herself Bonnie Elizabeth Parker, dating her birth to October 1st, 1910 and her death to May 3rd, 1934. Because she didn't need to narrate Bonnie and Clyde's story, because it was history. She didn't need to explain who she was, she was known, and above all, she knew herself. There's another one about how she named herself Amaryllis because of the bouquet she'd first laid eyes on in her hospital room, or September because of the month she'd first open her eyes in. These stories are the sponge, soap and water washing at last the black crosses off my arm. Ash tattoos marks of memories over the old figures of the forgotten. A gun, a flower, a gold bar, signs and symbols of their history covering the anonymous X of each story. My arm becomes a colorful mosaic where distinct and dissimilar parts intermingle into one piece. I don't have a tattoo for myself on that limb amongst all of their tattoos. My story doesn't need to be sketched, it's already been pencilled and painted on my thigh. Before me, before all of the Jane Does before me. It's the tattoo of a doe, not browsing nor bouncing but staring straight at you, as if standing in the headlights of your car, as if waiting for the collision, waiting for the twenty-three collisions. That one is mine;

elbows supporting heavy heads and furrowed foreheads have worn off a few shades of the armrests' brown cotton. The couch's cushions haven't outlasted children's jelly fingers and dogs' muddy paws without smears or scratches, but the scars on the couch's fabric have been carefully tucked under a clean quilt. Just like the mother before me wears her wrinkles on her face, but covers the bumps of her noodle necklace underneath her dainty dress. Once again, she sits on the edge of the same seat, presenting the same tea and providing the same biscuits, repeating the same story to similarly unwanted guests, but this time, this one time, to a wanted guest. It's the story of Lucy. Driving down for the weekend. Visiting her parents for a couple of days. She needs time away from the city, to think, to talk. And the night is calm, without traffic, without pouring rain or howling wind, but the storm is inside the car. For in there, Lucy isn't just a lost daughter, Lucy is also a wife and a mother. Though after the accident, she doesn't wake up with her husband, she doesn't wake up with her daughter either, and she doesn't ever really wake up herself. Only a stranger with a doe tattooed on her thigh does, whispering, weeping, and wailing about a *doe*;

" – and that's your mom's story of her sweet Lucy, that's not the story of my Luce," Ash sneers. "She was lost. She wanted a tattoo, and she wanted more than a tattoo. I came up with the idea of the doe. Because of her big brown eyes, dilated by dread and danger. It means nothing, Doe. It never meant anything. But she kept her tattoo and the guy who'd done her tattoo silent. She slept with her secrets until she couldn't sleep anymore. So she tried running away. You know the rest. Car, crash, and amnesia. She'd run away, she could close her big brown eyes and she could sleep again. But she came back. Wanting a black cross tattooed on her skin to remember her older self, while not wanting to take the medicine keeping her remembering. She was a hypocrite, and all of them were hypocrites, coming back cross after cross only to run away. Until you, Doe. You remembered and you helped everyone else to remember. You gave them back their names, but you didn't give one to yourself. And I know you're tired, you've lived too many lives, so live your own life. Don't prepare the next one, don't put her name on that bank account, or on that driving license, or on that car. Don't forget. Because I want you, not another one of them. Please take those pills and remember. Please;

"look a doe! Mom, look! Dad, look, Dad!" My white knuckles straining around the steering wheel, my husband shouting, my daughter squealing and straining to reach the window, unbuckling her seatbelt, her father unbuckling his own seatbelt, clutching and clasping at the leather under my hand, pressing the pedal under my foot, pushing farther and faster away from the doe, looking down at the speed, looking up at the doe in the middle of the road. The breaks. The screeches. The tumble. Two unbuckled empty seats. One buckled seat. Glancing out of the horizontal windshield to the vertical world, seeing a doe, staring at me, springing around, skipping away, and I forget

Lucy Grace

Lucy Grace writes fiction in the UK. Her short fiction and flash has been shortlisted and longlisted in a number of competitions including the Bridport Prize, Fish, and EllipsisZine Awards, and was the winner of the 2018 Writers & Artists Yearbook Short Story Award. In 2019 her debut novel was listed in the Lucy Cavendish Debut Novel Award and she is trying to finish it off as quickly as possible. Her work has been published in several print anthologies and online, and can be found online at lgracewriter.wordpress. com or on Twitter @lgracewriter

Sand Seven

When she woke in the early morning the brother was asleep on the ground. He had pulled the plastic over his head and it was weighted down at the bottom. He lay shrunken inside, the sheet sucking in and blowing out with his breath.

The sister moved her lower jaw and grit ground against her teeth. She spat out thick saliva and looked to see if the brother was alive, but her slitted eyes were sore with the sand. They had left the house three days ago when it came again, but now it was time to go home. The father had been left behind – he was a difficult man and refused to travel, but the brother and sister knew it was best. They could not have brought him up here, he would have slowed them down.

"I think it's turning now."

The wind that blew the sand in was warm and predictable. The brother was always surprised by it, then he always assured the sister it would be the last time, but she knew this was bullshit. He spoke a lot of bullshit. She had been looking forward to him leaving home, but of course that was before. He would not leave now.

"Get up."

The sister kicked the brother in the back with the pointed toe of her boot and he uncurled like a crab, stretching the plastic. She looked out across the valley. They had walked up the steep side and found a place near the top, in the lee of a warmed stone embankment. To the left was an indentation in the sandstone rock, a hollowed out small cave perfect for protection, but she had told the brother they would not shelter inside. It had a single opening and stank of piss, only defending from the weather. As a child she could remember long summers playing here. Julia would dare her to go into the darkness, and the sister rubbed her forearms as her fine blonde hairs stood on end, feeling the sudden chill in the shadow. Once they had found a charred space in the dirt, in the centre of a circle of black feathers. Between each feather was a single gleaming bone, porcelain pale, like fingers on piano keys without the flesh. As their eyes adjusted and they bent to look something moved in the dark of the cave and they turned and ran, heaving on desperate legs until they reached Judith's lawn, and lay under the sprinkler on a thousand tiny green swords and laughed at their breathlessness. They did not visit the cave again.

There was no movement on the hillsides. She could not see much through her glasses – they were scratched almost opaque – but the valley floor was still concealed beneath clouds of crimson sand. A scarf wound over her ears and around the lenses, binding them to her head and allowing no entry points for tiny grains. She wore a white face mask over her nose and mouth, and it was sandstained blood red where she breathed.

The brother had scrabbled in his bag for the coverings and was trying to fix them around his head. He was still under the plastic, but it was lifting at one corner and she knew the sand would already be inside.

"Come on."

The sister kicked him again and took a few steps away, her face pointed down the valley to their home. From up here she could see whole houses, roofs of houses and then just chimney pots. She looked for the liquorice strip that was the road back, uncoiling down the hillside like a moving snake beneath the blowing sand, and tried to measure how far they could get by walking. It would be easier now most of the sand was behind them.

"Pick up your stuff, then."

The sister had already hefted her pack onto her back, wrapped in its plastic, and started off with her head down. The brother was scrambling around trying to stuff things into his pack and he followed with staccato steps, hurrying to keep up.

"Will it be safe to go back?" he asked.

"How do I know?"

"Will he still be there? Will he be okay?"

The sister walked more quickly and didn't answer. She heard his question but didn't have anything to say.

When they were a third of the way from the bottom of the valley, the black tarmac began to disappear under the shifting grains. At first it was just blowing in light drifts across the road surface, but after a few minutes more all black was gone.

"We're too early," said the sister. "We'll have to wait."

"But what about him?" asked the brother.

"What about him?" said the sister, without expression.

She turned off the road towards a house with a porch. At the side of the house was a shed and she went over to it. She pulled hard at the door but the sand on the floor blocked the door from opening and she had to scrape it away with her boot. The gap grew wide enough for her to slide in sideways without her pack, which she pulled in after her.

"Come on," she said to the brother. The brother took off his pack and slid through the narrow space. It was easier for him, without breasts.

Inside the gloom of the shed were two garden chairs, crouched on top of each other, and a folded black bat of a parasol. She set the two chairs out and sat in one, her pack on the floor. Even in the shed she did not remove her coverings; the grains of sand were still blowing in the air.

"How long do we wait?" asked the brother.

"Until we can see the houses at the bottom of the valley," she replied. "We'll listen."

They sat without speaking but the noise was maddening. The warm wind blew sand relentlessly against every surface; it hissed against the metal roof sheets and spattered on the boarded-up window. The sister thought of a high-school trip to Niagara Falls, and how she could not hear Julia over the roar of the water. This was a nightmarish version of that, the sand a dry, gritted, painful substitute for water. This was hell.

The sister sat briefly with her eyes closed but this magnified the sound. Opening them, she looked at the brother staring fixedly at the door of the shed. Even through his glasses she could see the run of tears, although she could not tell if they were from emotion or the sand. It did not matter – weeping was not cleansing now. Tears were choked with salt and caused painful welts on delicate cheeks. The brother's face was already scoured red. He did not need to rub the tears for them to hurt.

They sat for at least three hours, maybe more. The sister could not tell how long but it seemed to be about that. She looked at her watch all the same. Some habits still continued from then. She had been very proud of her watch, before. It was from the high-end jeweller in the city, a present from herself to herself, bought with her first pay packet, from a shop with a doorbell and a fake glass entrance where you had to wait whilst the door behind you locked and the door in front of you unlocked. It was to stop robbers, but the sister felt exposed whilst waiting in the glass cube, as though she were in an x-ray machine and everyone could see inside her. Her face was flushed when the inner door opened, and as she stepped into the shop it had taken her a moment to gain her senses.

The watches were oversized and heavy on her birdbone wrist, but she did not care. She had felt alarmingly adult in her first week at work and needed something weighty to hold her down. The steel bracelet bound her to the earth. It had cost almost an entire month's wages, but as she was still living at home, she could afford it. The salesman instructed her – if she tightened the little wheel properly the watch was proofed for 100m below the ocean's surface – there was no way in for water, the tiny seals kept all moisture out.

They had not known then about the sand.

When the early grains began to blow in the air, one of the very first had slipped under the crown and settled in, waiting for her to wind it. As she loosened the little wheel the grain slid into place, holding the metal apart like an open door. More grains came on in, more and more of them until there were enough to stop the watch movement from scraping its way around the dial, and time was stopped one evening at eight forty-three. There was no significance to this, but there was to the watch, and the sister felt the sharp edges of the bezel under her fingertips whilst she considered time passed. It was relative now.

"Let's go, then," she said, standing up and brushing sand from her thighs. She spat again onto the floor, but there was no moisture in her mouth, so the glob clung to her lips, refusing to move.

"There must be a tap."

She pushed at the shed door, but it did not move. Outside, the sand had piled up and she could not open it. The brother stood up and gave it a hard shove with the side of his body and it moved an inch or two. The light outside was reddening and the sister knew they would have to walk quickly.

"Do it again," she said, "harder."

The brother gave the door a few more shoves until there was about a six-inch gap.

"You go, you're skinnier," said the sister. The brother went sideways through the slit and she heard the scraping sound of the sand outside. In a moment or two, the door was pulled a little wider and she pushed quickly through the opening, her left shoulder catching painfully on the wooden edge of the door, but she did not make a sound.

"Tap," said the brother, pointing.

They walked over to the side of the house and adjusted the packs on their backs. The girl cracked a plastic bottle as she turned the stiff mechanism. With an empty grinding sound dirty water dripped from the lip. She bent and covered the spout with her mouth, catching the muddied drops on her tongue and rolling them around before spitting into the empty flowerbed. It was warm but she did not care. She watched the drops fill the bottle an inch before screwing on the lid.

"Your turn."

The brother gave her room to step back before bending. He was taller than she and steadied himself with his hand on the tap whilst he wet his mouth. He did not fill his bottle, and she did not remind him. He was old enough to remember these things by himself, and she was not his parent.

As he straightened, she was already at the roadside, looking down the now black strip winding to the bottom of the valley.

"Come on," she said. "There's not much time." And they set off together along the road.

It was difficult to walk on the fine moving sand underfoot. They passed no other travellers – there was barely anyone left in this part of the town now. They did not hold hands. It had been a few years since they had touched each other at all, and the thought of it was too strange. They had not been particularly close as children, even when the mother was here, but when the sand started, and the mother and little sister were gone, they moved far away from each other.

The brother walked behind the sister. He copied her rhythm and moved at her pace. Whilst she was leading, he did not need to look up or around, and he concentrated on the pack on her back. Hanging from the zip was a yellow pineapple keyring made from beads. She had had this as long as he could remember, it must have been from school. He only had a fleeting memory of her at school as she was nine years older. It was best, for him, although he did not know it, that people did not realise they were the sister and the brother of each other. She was fiercely bright, far cleverer than him, and people wouldn't have liked it.

The sister stopped and turned, the pineapple swinging.

"We'll go this way and along the back fence. We'll be able to see from there."

The brother nodded under his coverings, but he needn't have bothered. She wasn't asking him. Already she had changed direction and was off along the path.

At the house she went through the gate and up to the door at the back. Her hand slipped on the brass door knob and she wiped the sand from her palm onto her jeans and tried again. The door grated open; it was stiff and did not move freely.

"Father?"

The sister called out into the silence. She stepped on the razor edges of the cracked lino as she went into the kitchen. The brother could not see her, and he felt alone. He quickened his pace to be close enough to touch her hair in its bindings.

"We're home."

The sister was not asking a question now, she had already taken the pack from her shoulder and reached for the water bottle. It was difficult to see in the room – the sand had etched the window glass and created a red fog. The brother hated it, he felt as though he were inside a body, suffocating. He pushed the living room door too hard and it banged into the wall, surprising her.

"Jesus," said the sister. "What the fuck are you doing? Be useful, for Christ's sake."

The brother knew the routine. There had been seven sands now, each longer than the one before, and they were more used to dealing with it. They knew it came with the fullest moon and they knew it would leave when the tides called. They did not know where it came from – no one did. The grains disrupted the satellite messages and wrapped the radio signals in rolling red clouds until they were silenced. After sand two, the bloodied sky retreated from the surface but continued to roll above the earth, bouncing communications out into deep space and rendering the satellites useless. No one had expected that, to be made silent by blowing sand. People were having to learn how to live again.

The sister did not know how long she could exist here. She watched the brother as he crouched on the tiles, emptying his pack in a pile on the floor. He looked up at her, a motherless boy.

"What's for dinner?"

"What about father?" she asked.

The brother looked guilty and rose to his feet. He had pulled the wrappings from around his face and they lay untidily around his neck like sticky bandages from fetid wounds.

"He'll be all right, he always is."

"Let's see to him first."

They climbed the stairs together to the bedrooms. All the doors were closed, and plastic sheeting was taped to each frame. The covered door at the far end was the father's room. Plastic hung down to the floor and the sister bent down to peel it away. She opened the door and went in, holding her breath against the sour male smell. The curtains were closed but she knew the geography of the room well enough to take five paces to the foot of the bed. Over the bed was another tented canopy made from plastic sheet, a rustling Bedouin tent. The brother was at the window, opening the curtains, but there was little light at this end of the day, made less by the sand etched glass and the plastic taped over the frame.

"Father?"

The sister moved around the bed to the side table. It lay cluttered with medicines and pill bottles, some on their side, some pills spilled out onto the wooden top. There was an empty glass, several lidless water bottles and a pair of scratched spectacles.

"Father."

The sister reached out, her fingers touching the plastic. It moved under her touch like thin skin.

"Father."

The sister pulled her hand back and rested it at her throat. The figure in the bed was silent and still in a manner that told her life had left it a while ago. He was fifty-eight.

The brother was still at the window, cursing the stiff sash. The sister turned and walked out of the room, along the hallway, down the stairs and out of the front door. She only stopped walking when she reached the middle of the street, where she crouched down with her back to the house. From the window the brother saw her and did not dare to turn around.

"Father," he said, but he already knew. Then he was running down the stairs on child's legs, down the path to his sister huddled in the street. He was crying noisily, mucus blowing in bubbles from his nostrils as he reached down for his sister on the ground.

"He's dead, it's Father, oh God, what are we going to do, he's dead, he's dead. Do something, something, oh God."

Whilst he was crying and wailing the sister was still. On the road in front of her a line of ants was making its way from underneath the kerbstone to a clump of grass. Each following the other, the ants moved single-mindedly with a purpose she recognised. She was a leader; she had tolerated her high-school friends who talked incessantly about proms and weddings and babies. She could think of nothing worse than to belong to an unlistening man, a man who would slow her down and stop her moving. She had made plans to leave. She had not decided where – she trusted she would know she was at the place when she reached it – but she knew that to leave was to lead and that was all she wanted. Until the mother and sister left first and cheated her. One day, they were gone, and she was still here, trapped with the men who didn't want to admit they needed her to lead. They had each stolen her life from her, and she would never forgive them.

The sister leaned forward and put a big stone in the path of the ants, crushing them dead. Those behind in the line moved uncaringly around the broken bodies and continued onwards. She stood up and flexed her ankles, tipped up and back on her toes. The brother was still weeping on his knees in the road. She looked down at him and shook her head. She could not help him now.

The sister had known this time would come. Each time the sands came, she left more of the father's medicine within his reach, hoping. At this seventh sand she had left less water too; when the brother was already on the road, she pretended she needed to pee and had gone back upstairs. The father had been lying in the plastic tent, and as she entered the room, he turned his face away. He had not spoken to her for the five months since the mother and little sister left.

"Goodbye, Father," she had said at the beginning of this seventh sand, but made no attempt to touch him or look him in the eye. She felt nothing. She had checked the window tape, closed the door, sealed the plastic and put the towel across the gap at the bottom. She knew he would be all right – it was a method they had all used at the start, but the thickening darkness was too much for her and she had decided to move out to higher ground each time it came. At their house in the bottom of the valley the sand had blown against the sealed doors and windows until they were entombed inside, buried alive inside a family coffin. She knew after the first sand that she could not survive it again, and when she returned home after the second sand the mother and the little sister were gone, and the father silent.

Back in the house she found her pack where she had left it. She filled four water bottles, collected six small discs of tinned fish and biscuits from the cupboard and rolled a blanket from the sofa, tying it with the curtain cord. Whilst she was doing this the brother came in and sat at the table with his head in his hands. Neither of them spoke. The brother could feel her.

"Don't leave me with him," he started, but didn't say anymore. The sister didn't reply.

She checked her watch. Eight forty-three. It could have been eight forty-three. Dusk was creeping around the edges of the garden. She would need a torch. The brother had not closed the back door when he came in, and as she walked out she did not touch it either. The sister left the air standing in the house, she left the brother sitting at the table, and she set off up the empty black road.

She took a different route to usual, following the fairy path she and Julia had used each summer on their way up the valley side to the cave at the top. She walked doggedly onwards, comforted in the gloaming, her fingers pressing the gold necklace charm in her pocket. The charm had been her mother's, a gift from one of the admirers at the late bar where she worked when the sister was at high school. The sister grimaced as she thought of her mother's tawdry satin blouses, gaping at her breasts when she leaned forward, of her laughing wetly and redly into the cheap whisky fumes of the sweating drinker in front of her. Shame burned the sister's face as she strode on. She pressed the meagre gilded bird between her finger and thumb until it marked the pad of her skin. The mother had never taken it off – she came home from the bar later than usual one night and there it was, mocking the rest of them with a single garnet eye. Everyone saw it and no one spoke of it, and the mother wore it around her neck for the rest of her life.

The sister had picked it up from the ground outside the cave. She had seen it gleaming in the sunlight – half buried in the sand, the garnet eye glinted like a drop of blood. The chain had been broken in the struggle and was missing, but the resilient, cheap golden bird remained, dented yet intact. The sister hated it. She had picked it up from the ground and held it so tightly in her fist that the jagged beak had pierced her palm, and she had opened her hand to see her blood resting with the garnet eye, and she did not feel anything.

She was almost at the top of the hill. Reaching into her jeans pocket, she took out the golden charm and swung her pack from her back. Her beaded pineapple had a keyring fitting, and she slid the hook of the charm alongside the cheap glass until both hung side by side. For a moment, she looked at them, until she was sure, and then she put her pack on her back again and began to walk. When she passed the cave, she did not look inside. She knew that the cave held only darkness, and she had had enough of that.

She was ready to learn to live again.

Rebecca F. John

Rebecca F. John is the author of one short story collection, *Clown's Shoes*, and one novel, *The Haunting of Henry Twist*, which was shortlisted for the Costa First Novel Award. Her short stories have been broadcast on BBC Radio 4. In 2015, her short story, *The Glove Maker's Numbers* was shortlisted for the Sunday Times EFG Short Story Award. She is the winner of the PEN International New Voices Award 2015, and the British participant of the 2016 Scritture Giovani project. In 2017, she was named on Hay Festival's 'The Hay 30' list. She lives in Swansea with her three dogs.

The Sea Thief

Must be it's the wind that steals the sea, she thinks, scraping and scooping the way it does here, in the crescent hook of the land. She does not know about the moon; its elliptical orbit; the gravitational attraction of the water to that neat, pale body. Never been permitted to step into the schoolhouse on Libanus Hill. Never opened a book. Suspects she knows nothing outside the clammy cold of her father's window panes and the buttery heat of her breath, misting against them.

She takes a step back, watches the patched mist chill then shrink then disappear. There is some logic to the reaction. She can neither fathom nor name it. When she steps forwards again, she holds her breath for as long as she can, one hand clamped over her mouth so that the callouses on her fingers scratch the softer skin of her lips.

Wait, Morwenna. Her lungs ache. Wait. Cannot let her breath obscure the expanse of exposed beach which fronts her father's house, or the first splay of light to break the flat grey predawn. She needs to see the women.

Every morning they come, wading out over the mudflat, baskets balanced on their heads. Off-shore squalls drag at their thick flannel skirts and shawls. The donkey plods behind them, nose low, head and tail swaying, tufty ears flickering against the weather. The women do not hunch like the donkey. They stand straight, tall, until they bend to their work.

Morwenna is captivated by the rhythms of their lives. Dreams of how it would feel, to stand on the mudflat, eyes tearing with the cold, hair whipped by the cross-shore, skin turned to gooseflesh. She's familiar with the scent of the sea. Knows it from the fish her father brings home and slaps on the kitchen worktop for her to gut and fry every Wednesday and Saturday: the bitter chill of deep darkness. But a scent is not enough. Morwenna yearns for something. Thinks it might be out there, amongst the women. Doesn't know. She lets enough breath escape to paint a ghost on the window pane, raises a fingertip to it, then changes her mind and looks past it.

The morning's light comes slow: a weak trickle through heavy pigeon-feather clouds. The women tread in its muted gold trail. Morwenna stands heart-still, hopes her father will not wake until she has watched the women raking and scraping the sand. But before they have reached their usual patch, the singular thunk of her father's feet hitting the floorboards as he swings out of bed sounds in Morwenna's chest: she is a drum he strikes with his endless crotchet-beat routines; hourly he sets her stretched skin to reverberating with his words, his orders, his refusals, his love, his pain.

Her only reprieve from his affection is to sleep, but Morwenna has nothing to fill her dreams. No adventure. No memories beyond the walls and chores of this house. No stories. Her life is shut behind a red front door whose brass knocker is pitted and dulled by the salt wind she feels against her skin only when she pegs the clothes out, every second afternoon. She pegs the clothes out even when it rains.

The floorboards in the next bedroom groan as her father inches unevenly towards the door. His knees lock overnight. The greater part of each morning is spent before the fire, knuckling them loose and grousing away the ache. When she watches him disappear down Stepney Road towards the pub at lunchtime, he pitches a few degrees to the left, his shoulder dipping into the pain. He drinks three pints and returns home a touch straighter, a trace softer. Except on those days when he stops at the cemetery. Those days, he misses her mother so badly he limps into the past and deposits all his words there. Sometimes, weeks lapse before he recovers them and Morwenna endures the silence inside the house by filling her dreams with noise. The noises the women hear.

She sleeps to windborne sand rasping in her ears. Her breath heaves in time with the rolling approach of the tide. The women laugh and shout instructions to the donkey and pass their secrets to each other on the airstream. They wash away her father's voice, his insistence that he must keep her close and safe. Morwenna closes her eyes to the sounds, waits for her father to reach his bedroom door and call out for her. Shapes their words as definitely as she does the bread dough she kneads before church on Sundays. She has deciphered enough, hooking her fingertips over the lip of the opened upstairs window, standing up on the sill, pressing herself to the glass to listen, to know how each of them speaks. To learn their names. To pretend they are hers.

Beti. Thirza. Mabli. Annie. Nest.

She breathes a blank page onto the window pane and traces out their individual letters. Or what she thinks might be the lines and curls of their letters. Never properly learnt her alphabet. The sounds hold distinct forms, though, inside her head.

Beti. Thirza. Mabli. Annie. Nest.

She recites the names like prayers. Listens. Marvels at the ease with which the women address each other. What a joy, to have friends to clown and argue with. To have a voice to share.

More and more, they talk about the men.

"How much longer do you think it can go on?" they wonder. "Does your Cadog write often? Does Jim? Does Llew?"

They dip away into their thoughts then – silent as swans tucking their heads beneath their feathers to sleep – where, Morwenna thinks, they visit their husbands.

This morning, Thirza is claiming to have seen Cadog. "I felt him in the dent of his usual armchair," she says. "Last night. I swear it. Smelled his musk in the hallway at the time he usually comes home from work."

She hears tears on Thirza's tongue and her own swell to match them. Doesn't want her lids to be swollen red when her father drags her from the window and onto the landing to help him downstairs, so she screws them shut, holds her breath, listens until she hears, above the rush and sway of the sea, Thirza describe how brilliantly blue Cadog is, how she sees him always surrounded by colour, as though his shadow is a rabble of common blue butterflies, wings forever ruffled in the form of her husband, and how she glimpses that exact shade reflected in the last rivulets of tide as it washes away some mornings, and the words shine like silver in Morwenna's head, and she shuts her eyes tighter, holding to the darkness so that, against it, she might see the colours more clearly.

"Morwenna," her father calls. She doesn't answer, can't. She's on the mudflat, lying on her back, arms thrown out, legs spread, so that she is star-shaped. A child's idea of a star. Wet sand clumps against the back of her head, tangling her hair, but she does not want to stand. She is comfortable, pinned down by the weight of her clothes as the last shimmer of water to slick the sand seeps into the wool of her skirt and shawl. She is happy. It is Beti, Thirza, Mabli, Annie, Nest, and

Morwenna now. It ought to be. She understands, thinks she does, what Thirza means when she says she sees Cadog's colours. The women are colours in the veined dark behind her eyelids.

Thirza is the soft, pearlescent pink of first or last light. Beti, the brightest white spark of a rearing wave's crest. Nest, the soft bronze shine of wet sand. Mabli, the hushed grey of a herring gull's wings. Annie, the opaline gleam of a pearl shell.

They would gather around and lean over her, were she really lying on the sand. Enquire whether she was hurt. Coax her upright. Brush the muck off her skirt. She's certain they would help her stand tall, if they knew.

"Morwenna!"

Eyes on the door, she snatches a desperate inhalation, holds it, then breathes it all over the window. Watches the glass crawl with steam. Lifts a forefinger. Draws her letters into it. She thinks they are the right ones. Hopes. They'll be gone soon, so it will hardly matter.

Turning away to answer her father's calls, Morwenna does not imagine what a cacophony the window pane will appear in the late afternoon sun, as it slants inland just so, to five curious passers-by. Cannot imagine that, from the outside, the light will catch all those curls and dips and lines her pointed finger has made and illuminate them into life again. Never learnt a single scientific fact. Doesn't know the effects of condensation. Would not dream that the word she has just drawn might show so clearly, a streaked and milky stain, for anyone to see and read and puzzle over. For anyone to act upon.

She steps onto the landing, gently closing her bedroom door behind her, believing she has silenced her scream. Thinks again about the wind: that flighted sea thief. Thinks herself as easily stolen. Doesn't imagine. Doesn't dream. Doesn't dare hope that the women might hear her.

Mubanga Kalimamukwento

Mubanga Kalimamukwento is a Zambian author, whose first novel, *The Mourning Bird*, won the Dinaane Debut Fiction Award (formerly the European Union Literary Award) and was published by Jacana Media. She won the Kalemba Short Story Prize 2019 in Zambia and was shortlisted for the SyncityNG Anthology and Prize in Nigeria. Her stories have been published in Zambia, Nigeria, Canada, USA, France, Singapore, South Africa and Australia. She's a lawyer by training, a mom of two and an LLM candidate at the University of Minnesota. She's also a Hubert H. Humphrey (Fulbright) Fellow (2018/2019) and a Young African Leadership Initiative Fellow (2017).

The Devil's Ivy

In the cramped living room of our tiny house, tucked in the middle of squalid Chelstone police camp, grew four devil's ivy, rooted in drab cement pots. Their lush leaves defied grim-brown walls and crept on dead lemon branches until they kissed the roof, luxuriously framing our tattered suede couches. Bamama, my mother, said I was just like those flowers, pretty but poisonous. When she wasn't polishing the scarlet cement floors, her long fingers were caressing the ivy leaves as she watered them.

Sometimes, as I watched her tending her plants, I wished that I was named Ivy instead of Maluba – Flowers. Perhaps then, Bamama would have seen me as she did them: as tenacious blossoms in a lightless home instead of her forgetful and careless only daughter, a poor substitute for a son. Had I been Ivy, instead of Maluba, maybe then, she could've loved me too.

When I was eleven, I asked Batata, my father, why he chose my name. He said, "Because, baby, a flower is the most desired thing on earth." I didn't understand him then, but when he gave me the look – his hooded eyes searing through my navy school uniform, tracing the outline of my budding breasts, leisurely descending to the place where my widening hips met in a tuft of curly, coal-black hair – my armpits prickled with sweat and I recoiled, knowing to tuck my wish and question away.

For the flower which wasn't an ivy, Bamama didn't prune her harsh words or caress the vine. Instead, it was, "Stop screaming and let me comb your hair. We are late for church!"

So, the day she died, I half expected relief and not the stabbing pain in my chest and the rock in the back of my throat. Bamama was clad as she would on any other Wednesday, in her pristine white nurse's uniform and midnight-leather loafers. But, unlike her patients at Kanyama Clinic, she had no lingering sickness and couldn't even give me a farewell rebuke like: "*Kasambe!*" Go and take a bath! "You are too playful for your own good!"

Instead, Bamama died like a storm in mid-October: one moment gushing, quelling a blazing summer, the next, hauled into a still, dead calm, not even a puddle where she had once been. I was twelve by then, and she was forty-two.

I had planned repeatedly to tell her about Batata's secret ritual, but whenever she found me playing on the floor and greeted me with, "Close your legs!" and a pinch of my ebony thighs, I decided against it, knowing she would only blame me.

But then, one day, returning early from a two-night shift, she'd finally found him, pinning me down as he ripped into me. I was clawing at the cloud of sheets on my thin mattress to suppress the urge to scream. In the background, an eagle was announcing noon on Zambia's National Broadcasting Corporation. My eyes blurred over as I stared at a ray of sunlight seeping through a tiny hole in the roof when Bamama let out a small cry, making her presence known. Her voice tore through the room like thunder.

Batata pulled out abruptly, the folds of his neck mirroring the stems of the ivy twisted around dry branches. He scrambled for his trousers, breathlessly spitting, "Insolent. Stupid. B-b-bitch," but Bamama stopped him with a perfect aim of her loafer.

His eyes flew wide as she charged him in an explosion of useless blows, fighting him for the first time, but his powerful punches crushed her anger into silence.

"The time is now twelve-ten on the second of July 2008, and you are listening to the lunchtime news. President Levy Patrick Mwanawasa has been flown to Paris after suffering a stroke in Egypt where he was attending an African Union summit," droned the newsreader while Bamama's voice ceased.

Batata stood back for a moment, rubbing his balding head and darting his eyes between Bamama and me. I watched in silence as he carried her limp body into the street where people looked away as they walked.

Eventually, a navy Corolla stopped for him.

"Please, my wife is sick, I need to take her to the hospital," Batata pleaded.

The driver looked sceptical but dared not refuse to help a uniformed policeman and a sick nurse.

"We are going to the University Teaching Hospital. Hurry."

Somewhere on that seventeen-kilometre drive to the emergency room, Bamama died.

While I waited for their return, I rubbed the bean between my legs, wincing because it still stung, but pining for his words, "Beautiful flower."

I wandered into the sitting room and stayed there until Aunt Beene, Bamama's half-sister, arrived, long after sunset. Her wail confirmed my fears and informed the neighbours to come and finally grieve for my mother.

Those who came took the furniture out into the yard to make room for more mourners, leaving the sitting room hollow but for the rich ivy in each corner. In the vacuum, the beautiful leaves turned ugly. They, like me, had been silent witnesses to my mother's misery.

Over the big one next to the door, he had strangled her once until a steady trickle of yellow seeped through her clothes. Near the one that framed the window, he had broken her arm one Christmas Eve, for opening the door too late for him. Near the one by my bedroom, he had punched her in the abdomen until her uniform and the floor were the same blood red.

After each beating, came apology day. Bamama would rise before the sun to cook him a steaming bowl of mealie porridge and fermented milk.

"Breakfast, *Bauhi Maluba.*" *Breakfast, Maluba's father,* she would say, as she knelt to serve him, edging away from the low wooden table. She added the last part to her routine after the time she accidentally spilt some porridge on his feet, and he kicked the table at her, leaving a lightening-like memory of the day on her left arm.

Since then, Bamama had perfected her apologies, waiting until he had the first spoonful in his mouth before she walked out of the room.

After the apology breakfast, he would walk to Chelstone Market and buy her a gift. A cabbage, his favourite, for her to cook the apology dinner. If I squinted my eyes just right, the round vegetable resembled the sunlight-yellow flower which the ivy bloomed in winter.

That Batata, the one who broke bones and burnt arms with his food, and the one of Bamama's week-long funeral were not the same. The way he wept into his ashy fingers those five long days, I almost sympathised with him, as the other mourners did. Almost.

"He is depressed, eh?" a woman asked.

"At least now he can have a son," responded another.

Chuckles.

"Ah, but how will he care for the girl?"

The girl. Two razor-sharp words.

"Not to worry, eh, he will manage. He is now an Inspector."

At night, I felt the blades of the question cutting into my sleep, denying me peace. *Who will take care of the girl?* I tossed and plotted my escape.

Maybe, I can sneak into one of the cars and buses lined outside the house and jump out wherever they stop. Maybe, I should run away, while playing a game of hide and seek with my friends. Maybe at the burial, I can slip through the crowd as they disperse. Maybe...

But when morning came, I lost my courage and hovered in the kitchen which still smelled of bleach and methylated spirits, like Bamama's uniform.

"Poor girl," one said.

"Eat your food," chimed another, clicking her tongue.

"He has a good job. He can take care of the girl." Those razors again.

After four nights of staying up, planning and failing, came burial day on day five.

We buried her at the edge of Leopard's Hill Cemetery, next to a long line of old graves with broken crosses and faded words. IP instead of RIP. ORN instead of BORN. Batata's workmates, police officers, in navy and green, lowered her glowing, white coffin into the ground, leaving Bamama's swollen face and battered body to feed the thorn bushes and trees that lined the dusty graveyard streets.

The cemetery was full. Auntie Rachael, Batata's friend, the one who accompanied him to the bars on Fridays, stood at the back, in a flower-print *chitenge* head wrap. Near her, stood Uncle Chishimba, from church, the one who came after every fight to counsel Bamama about respecting her husband. Bridget, the maid from next door, was inconsolable on a sunset-brown reed mat near me; she had begged Bamama to leave after each beating. Then there was Lucy, Bamama's workmate, sobbing silently under a tree. Her husband, Sergeant Mayaba, was comforting my grief-stricken father.

It felt like forever before the speeches ended and Pastor Mwape stood to read a Bible verse: "The life of mortals is like grass; they flourish like a flower of the field; the wind blows over it, and it is gone, and its place remembers it no more." A ripple of fresh weeping followed.

After the prayer, The United Church of Zambia choir – women, dressed in black skirts and blood-red shirts, burst out in a song. *Hush! Blessed are the dead.*

Finally, Batata rose. The sun, sinking towards the earth, darkened his pale features as he loomed over me. He took my hand to place a wreath of crimson roses on Bamama's grave. The wreath had an iris in the middle, as yellow as a ripe mango. If I squinted just right, it was the bud of the devil's ivy that mother loved so.

Not a cabbage for a meal this time.

When Batata's shaking hands brushed mine, it dawned on me: mother's shift, this time, was eternal. I finally broke down.

"It's okay, beautiful flower," Batata said between sobs, "Daddy is here."

The words, beautiful flower, unlocked memories of him stalking my bedroom at night. His fingers, tracing my skin in the dark. His hands, forcing my legs open. His hot breath over my guava-hard breasts. His groan as he plunged into me.

The next morning, I woke up courageous and knew what to do. I raced into the kitchen and said, "Let me serve him," to Auntie Beene, who was about to give Batata a bowl of porridge.

I had spent all night cutting ivy leaves and squeezing the milky mucous into a metal teacup until it was full.

"Please," I added, my resolve crystallised.

"Okay, dear. You are growing responsible," she said.

Women nearby nodded.

"Yes, auntie," I agreed, smiling. "I know just how he likes it."

"Breakfast is ready, Batata," I said, choking at the sound of my voice, an echo of Bamama's, smooth as avocado flesh. I knelt, slowly, next to a stool by his side, and set the plate down.

"*Ndalumba*." *Thank you*, he said, his voice gritty and hoarse.

I waited for him to receive my gift. Mealie porridge with enough fermented milk to mask the taste of poison.

"Thank you, baby," he repeated, hand shaking as he took the bowl. With his copper-brown eyes, he drank me in, pausing on my breasts and then plunging towards my crotch. The look. My pits prickled.

"Lovely girl," someone said.

Batata took the plate and slurped a spoonful of porridge.

I smiled, feeling the rock in my throat dissolve.

He devoured the rest of the porridge while I waited for him to start coughing and foaming before I edged away. The pain in my chest eased, and I opened my mouth. I walked past the lemon tree, letting poison drip out of me in a brittle laugh. I breezed past the hedge that fenced our little house. Raced past stationary cars through the winding line of mango trees that led to Great East Road, desperately hoping that I had used enough to turn him into nourishment for the thorns and trees in the cemetery, just like *Bamama*.

Sonal Kohli

Sonal Kohli grew up in Delhi and now lives in Washington, D.C. with her husband and daughter. She holds an MA in Creative Writing from the University of East Anglia. She was a recipient of the Bianca Pancoat Patton Fellowship at Sangam House. Her work has appeared in *Blackbird, Monkeybicycle, The Caravan, Unthology 7*, and was shortlisted for the Fish Short Story Prize 2014. Sonal is completing her book of interconnected stories that follows three generations of a post-partition immigrant family in Delhi, its servants, tutors, cousins and lovers, their loneliness, aspirations and small-scale industrial ambitions. www.sonal-kohli.com

The Outing

You get off the rickshaw at the banyan outside the post office. From here you plan to find Sister Celina's house on foot. You've applied Band-Aids to the back of your feet where the ballerinas bite. You wear a cream blouse and checked green skirt, hair in a small ponytail, the size of a shaving brush.

You walk past the tiny watch repair shop, the chow mein stall and its sizzling wok. You side-step a pile of dung. A puppy nibbles at cabbage leaves under a vegetable cart. Women with powdered necks and fresh lipstick haggle over the prices of brinjals and shiny tomatoes. The sounds of Super Mario Bros. – a ding, the mushroom popping – seep from the grimy curtain of the videogame parlour. Children surround the Kwality cart that's lit fluorescent green. In the mornings and afternoons when the school bus rolls through, the market is sleepy, but now it's overcome with a busyness that you find intoxicating. You live in an industrial area not far from here, next to the steel factory your family owns. No ice cream carts pass outside your house, no popcorn, no golgappawalas, only lumbering trucks, weary labourers. You spend your evenings playing table tennis against the veranda wall, or embroidering with grandmother, who you like and dislike in turns, and after the factory closes for the day sit on the swing that the

139

watchman's son has slung from the neem. When the watchman's son sees you, he withdraws to his shack. The watchman allows him outside the factory precincts to fetch tea, to simply cycle, and who knows maybe he comes as far as the market. You had to make your outing today sound official in order to wheedle permission out of your father, who can be very strict depending on his mood. A man's peeing against the low boundary wall of the cinema. You avert your eyes and quicken your step. Sister Celina's house lies somewhere beyond the market.

Celina was your senior, when you were in the second grade, she was in the tenth. You remember a cold morning when the bus broke down and the girls marched schoolward, she held your hand on one side and another little girl's on the other. Last summer Sister Catherine introduced her at the afternoon assembly as the ex-student who had returned to the school as a nun. Standing on the lawns, you were startled to see her in the white habit and veil, the cross in a plain black thread resting on her chest. You felt a twinge of sadness. Sister Celina became your Chemistry instructor. She paced as she taught, palms clasped, the rope-like veins on the back of her hands evincing an inner strength. She was not an engaging teacher, but she was not stern, and if a girl forgot to bring her textbook, she lent her her own. The textbook was unmarked, she didn't even note her name on the cover and it made you think how on Sports Day she would board the bus in the afternoon with her medals, strung through satin ribbons of red, yellow, aquamarine, still around her neck. You wonder often if she had any inkling back then that she would one day become a nun. After the Christmas break, Mrs. Nair once again took charge of the Chemistry lessons. Sister Celina was no longer seen in the staffroom, and not even on the teal van that ferried the nuns to and from the convent. It was heard she had undergone gallbladder surgery and was recuperating.

But as two months slipped by, there were whispers she got pregnant and ran away with a priest. It was a trite slander about a nun, and though everyone discussed it, not many trusted it to be true. On the way to a debate competition, the team learned from Mrs. Bakshi that actually Sister Celina had an argument with Sister Catherine and was overnight transferred to Paharganj to work with the city's orphans. Mrs. Bakshi is jealous of anyone who has the principal's affections. Her transfer theory remained uncorroborated. These days it is being passed about that Sister Celina joined the order after a heartbreak and having recovered has returned to her old life. She works at a pathology lab in Moti Nagar, it is said, and has been seen in short skirts and heels. You find yourself thinking about her when you work in the Chemistry lab; while you stand in the doorway that connects the house with the factory, watching the sky grow pale and labourers trickle out through the rust coloured gate; as you clean your teeth with a neem twig before bed. You're perplexed by the turns her life has taken. Like everyone you're curious about her disappearance, but your parents would be proud how you've kept away from gossip.

A woman waters the twin plants on her gatepost. You pass a crammed stationer run out of a house front. The market has petered out. Boys squat in the dirt shooting marbles. The rickshawala who rode you here passes by on the other side of the road, spokes sounding tinnily. You look back: The factories puffing smoke in the distance, tall dark chimneys against the mango sky, seem mythical.

There's nothing remarkable about the lane to your left, but its trees with the cables nestling in the tops and the yellow and pink apartments that give it an overall salmon hue seem to fit with your memory. You turn down it. In the lane, a pair of girls play badminton and you think of asking them if the Thomases live somewhere here, but two boys lean against a scooter watching the girls and you feel shy. You are shy of boys, they make you stutter. You walk on observing the apartments. The drains give off a salty green smell that's not wholly unpleasant. Some mornings when Celina was late for the bus, you saw her dash out of her lane, fast as P. T. Usha, while her father hurried after her with her lunchbox. How ordinary that moment was, how beguiling, you think now, Sister Celina was just a girl late for school. You sigh. You rub the back of your right foot where the ballerina is digging in just above the Band-Aid.

Railway Apartments, four storeys high, an exposed cement staircase that looks like a vertebrate, could be Sister Celina's building. You glance to check and it seems like the right distance from the mouth of the lane. The shuttlecock has landed close to the boys and the one in the baseball cap offers it to the girls, as though it were a rose. Even from where you stand you can hear the girls giggle. You open the rickety gate of the building and cross its dusty compound. You climb the cement stairs, nervous, palm clammy against the bannister. On the upper floor, you pick the furthest of the five doors and ring the bell. You clear your throat, wipe your palms on the checked skirt. The woman who answers the door smells of caramelised onions, has a spatula in hand. In response to your question, she scolds you for ringing the bell. You flush. You stop by the parapet to compose yourself. The sun has dimmed, the trees appear darker. The shuttlecock thwacks back and forth. You inspect above your heel to find a sore spot. You touch its peeling edges. Downstairs the rickety gate creaks. You glance over the parapet. You squint. You slip your foot back into the ballerina. Is it her? Is it? It is her. It is odd seeing her in regular clothes, to witness her hair, the strands that have come loose from the plait after a long day. She has grocery bags in both hands and a flabby black purse on one shoulder. She looks ordinary, like anyone one might pass in the street. Once again that twinge of sadness. She heaves a hand high enough to fasten the latch. Coriander peeps from a bag. Her footsteps on the stairs are quiet, reminding you of the thick-soled sandals she wore as a nun. Out of the corner of an eye, you glimpse her pass the landing and climb to the second floor. A door opens upstairs and then shuts. In the building across the lane a plump woman with a child on her hip calls out to a cobbler passing below. You tighten your little ponytail and turn toward the stairs.

Sister Celina appears at the door in a faded nightgown with white and blue flowers. She looks younger without the veil, face delicate, cheekbones pronounced. She has re-done her plait since coming home.

"May I come in please?"

For a second it seems like she'll send you away. Perhaps she doesn't like visitors. Perhaps she remembers you as the girl who spilled ammonium sulfide in the lab causing it to stink for days of rotten eggs. Something in her shoulders relents then. She gives a nod.

In the living room a woman's shelling peas. She looks at you as she slits a pod with her thumbnail and empties it into a bowl on the table. You say Hello and sit on the adjacent sofa. You hear Sister Celina open the fridge door in the kitchen. There's a TV trolley across from the sofas, the standby light of the VCR glowing. The day's washing rests on the back of a dining chair. The showcase is crammed with knick-knacks, framed photographs and old trophy cups. On one wall is a cross-stitch portrait of a woman by a pond, twilight shades of blue and purple. You would have expected to see in the house some sign of Sister Celina's recent nunhood, her habit and veil in a hanger, laundered, neatly ironed, yet to be put away, or at least a rosary on a side table, her cross. Instead there are these placid tokens of domesticity, the two women in their nightgowns and green dirt gathering under the mother's thumbnail. Sister Celina strikes a match in the kitchen, then another one, and finally the flare of the burner. When she returns, you'll start by introducing yourself. When she was teaching you, you didn't remind her you used to share a bus, for though you were once again in the same physical space, it felt she existed in a realm separate from yours. Now, however, at last, you can ask her about the nature of life. You will tell her about your dog, who drowned in the acid tank in the workshop, discovered only the next morning after the factory reopened; the pained sound the swing on the neem makes under your weight; your friend who after a summer in America returned with an accent, and forever altered. You want to know if Sister Celina had any intimation she would one day become a nun. And what caused her now to give up that path. You won't bring up the rumours, for they will unduly hurt her. Instead you will ask her if she thinks life in the end leads us to a happy place.

She comes to the living room with a soup bowl on a small plate, a steel spoon on the side. She moves the bag of peas to make room in front of her mother, spreads a napkin over her lap and gestures her to eat the soup. Sister Celina's eyes meet yours and, in their quietness, then the way she looks down, you sense there have been other visitors, with each of whom she has been respectful, as kind as possible. You want to hold her gaze to let her know you're not here to pry, but the mother is cracking open the pods now *crick-crick* instead of slitting them. Sister Celina tells her again to start with the soup and threads her way to the kitchen. A wisp of steam rises from the bowl and disappears. The cross-stitched woman gazing at the pink stars, it occurs to you, could be the art & craft project the girls do in the eleventh grade for Miss Betsy's class. You wonder if your parents will hang yours till years later, but they are not sentimental about keepsakes or about you for that matter. The mother continues to crack open the pods, frail wrists, hard knuckles.

Sister Celina returns with two tea cups on a tray and offers them to you. You take the one with croutons on top and leave the other that smells like coffee for her. She sits on the third sofa with her cup. She sips it, lips tight, back straight. You want to tell her the soup is good, tomato your favourite, but it's hard to start a conversation with the pods quacking and the mother's bowl growing steadily cold.

Sister Celina sighs and sets her cup on the table. She walks to the TV trolley, presses the keys on the VCR, then switches on the TV. The mother's heaved herself off the sofa. She hobbles to a switchboard and turns off the tube light. The room's dark now. The walls shift with colours from the screen. Ah, the mother's eating her soup. Sister Celina sips her coffee, more relaxed now, as though she's finally free to savour it. You too lean back into the cushions. The three of you watch the movie clustered around the table, as though it were something you did every evening. The movie is Indian but the characters speak English, the print grainy from being run over and over again. Miss Stoneham, who seems Sister Celina's mother's age, teaches Shakespeare at school and lives alone in her dilapidated apartment with her cat. Outside, the sun sinks and the moon pulleys up, the girls playing badminton return indoors, the rickshawala pedals home a passenger and his new mattress, the air smells damply of roses from the flower stall. Sister Celina fast forwards some scenes but the mother doesn't mind and you of course can't say anything. You fold your arms and marvel at the fact that you're here instead of at home, and you are surprised at yourself. *Itsy Bitsy Teenie Weenie Yellow Polkadot Bikini* plays on an old gramophone as Miss Stoneham's evenings liven up in the company of an ex-pupil and the pupil's boyfriend. Sister Celina sways her foot lightly. The coffee cup rests on the arm of the sofa, her flip-flop dangles from her toes. She appears at ease in her nightgown, on the sofa, in this TV lit house that smells of stale bread. The mother places her napkin and empty bowl on the table. You glance at the clock above the trolley. You pray your father is not back from the factory yet.

As Sister Celina sees you to the door, you find yourself searching for something to say. You notice the ballerina doesn't hurt anymore. "We used to ride the same bus to school," you say at last, "mine was the first stop in the mornings and yours the third, at the banyan. I wanted to tell you, I remembered you."

She smiles, nods.

You hail the rickshaw just as it is passing by, spokes sounding tinnily. The stationer has closed his shop, so has the tailor, the dhaba is full. Some stores have television sets turned on. The rickshawala veers to avoid a pothole. The approaching factories, tall chimneys against the night sky, don't seem so lonesome.

Rose McDonagh

Rose McDonagh was born in Edinburgh. Her writing has been published in a number of places including *New Writing Scotland, Gutter, SmokeLong Quarterly*, The Guardian online, *Brittle Star, The Nottingham Review* and *Reflex Fiction*. She won the Bath Flash Fiction Award and was shortlisted for the London Magazine Short Story Competition and the Dinesh Allirajah Prize. She has been a *Mslexia* guest blog author. She is a counsellor and currently works in community health. She is on twitter @rose_mcdonagh

Dog's Bone

I was a small child then and could hardly begin to understand what had happened. To me, it was the start of autumn, a time of wet gold leaves sticking to the bathroom skylight, green and black confectionery appearing in the village shop. My parents sheltered me from the television news and I did not use the internet unsupervised. Mr Webster, the shop's owner, bought in pumpkins, extra turnips and large bags of peanuts, like he did every year. The air had started to sweeten with the scent of wood smoke. We began using our own fireplace again and it came to be a focus of attention for me. I'd bring in twigs and leaves to throw into the flames, to watch them snap and spark. "Don't put too many wet twigs on, we'll get smoked out like bees," my mum said.

At school we were making a giant skeleton for Halloween. Papier-mâché bones glued onto a huge sheet of black card, placed into an outline the teacher had drawn. "Do you really think that's appropriate now?" one of the mothers asked our teacher at going-home time. There was a muffled conversation as I left, the two of them looking down at the half-formed skeleton, their hands on their hips.

"Why did she say that?" I asked my dad in the evening.

"I don't know, Elspie, she must have had her reasons."

Really I think I understood and was just checking my impression with an adult.

We carried on with our project. I liked making the bones out of newspapers and paste, shaping them like the dog toys they sold in the pet section of the store. In the end the skeleton had eighty two bones, we were proud of it and surprised to learn a real skeleton had far more.

Sometimes my parents talked about the news at home, we couldn't edge round it entirely. "It won't affect us here," my dad said, "It's happened very far away."

I began to drink hot milk at night like I used to when I was a much younger child. I'd sit up and watch nature documentaries with my mum, squashing in so close I was almost on her lap as pigmy elephants trotted across the screen. Or I'd play cards with my dad, snap or a simple version of black jack, leaving the table to drop a piece of kindling in the fire every now and again. We took to placing a lit candle between us while we played, silent gaps filled up with the ticking of the clock above us.

It wasn't long before people started to arrive from further south. First both the hotels were filled, every place taken on the caravan site, then people began to park cars and vans in the fields, setting up tents and paying a fee to the landowner. "It won't last forever," my dad said, "People are afraid they might get sick down south. Once all the fuss dies away, they'll go home. They'll have to go anyway when the cold sets in." We had a lot of new children to play with. They didn't go to the school, there wasn't room, but in the late afternoons and early evenings, the mix of us would gather in the park like baby goats collecting round a hay bale. There were always adults watching from the sidelines, a row of them marked by the shadow of the churchyard wall.

One day my mum and I were walking on the beach when we noticed that the sand up ahead of us appeared duller than usual. As we made our way further along, we realised half of the west bay was covered in dead sea creatures. They were mainly starfish, their bodies a pale grey or pink as cooked salmon. I crouched down to peer at their whorled limbs. Amongst them, there was an octopus with lightless, coin-sized eyes. I studied it closely then moved further in among the bodies. Once I'd got a few metres from my mother, I began to have a scrabbling sensation on my skin, as if the dead things were touching me. I started to take in small suctions of air, a kind of inverse scream. My mother took me by the hand and led me home. Later, I asked if the sea creatures had died because of the bomb and she said she didn't know. It could be a coincidence.

A word I was to notice a lot. In school, a girl sobbed because some of her hair came out as she was brushing it. "That's just a coincidence, hair falls out sometimes," the teacher said. Her voice was honey soft though the girl kept crying. "You've got a dog, Mhairi. You know how they shed big clumps of fur over the furniture? Well, humans lose a wee bit of hair now and again. It's so nice new hair has room to grow." Mhairi nodded, pinkeyed.

One night drinking my milk, I said to my mum, "I used to have a sippy cup." I remembered it, the blue top, how I'd chew on the spout with my teeth.

"When you were a baby."

"Can I have one now?"

"I don't think so love, they're for wee ones."

"I am a wee one."

"Not so much anymore. You're taller than me when you stand on a kitchen chair. Those cups are for wee ones who aren't at school yet."

I carried on sipping the warm milk from my mug. She watched me closely. "You could have cocoa in that if you want. Make it into a hot chocolate like you had in the café. I could put cream on top."

"I just want milk," I said.

Later I announced I'd buy a sippy cup from the local store with my pocket money. "That's up to you," my mum said.

The shop was attached to the post office and the next day when my mum was buying stamps, I searched the mugs and plates. They didn't have sippy cups in so I bought a dog's rubber bone toy instead. It was for the future, when we would have a dog, as my parents promised we would if ever one of them could work from home.

"That was sensible," my mum said after I showed her what I'd bought. The bone was pink, I reasoned it wouldn't matter if the dog was a boy since dogs were colour-blind. At that time my dad's job was to make deliveries all across the district. My mum worked in the office attached to the doctor's surgery and knew everyone's secrets.

"Can we get a dog if the school closes down?" I asked her. "I'd be at home to look after it then."

"Who said the school is closing down?"

"Just people." It was something I'd heard discussed many times now by parents, children, teachers.

"If the school closes down you'll have to go to the office with me or out in the van with dad."

"Not if your work closes down too," I said. I took the bone home and put it in my wicker basket of special things under my bed. From the window, I could see a dithering skein of geese going by. Below, the fields were full of brightly coloured tents. A few were now dotted amongst the heather further out.

The next day at school, during writing practise, a boy called Ruairi began making a thin keening noise. He was seated behind me. When I looked round I saw that he held one of his teeth in his palm. He rocked back in his chair, his hand out flat displaying it.

"It's a baby tooth," said one of the girls.

"It's not, it's not, that one fell out before and it growed back and it's fallen out again and it's not supposed to," he said. His palm closed up. He wiped his nose on the knee of his jeans. The teacher rose and guided him out of the class. She came back without him.

We carried on our writing. We were each to produce a story about a castle full of ghosts. I took a lot of care with that kind of thing, picturing the layout of the castle. Mine had three floors and many windows. At last, the bell rang for home-time.

"How was today?" my mum asked as we were walking back up the oak tree path. I leant my head against her, my feet still stepping forward. She always wore the same perfume from a diamond-shaped bottle, it was so much the scent of her that I was suspicious of anyone else who wore it, as if they had stolen some of her essence.

"We wrote about castles," I said. "Ruairi cried."

"What happened?"

"He got taken to the head teacher's." It was either that or the nurse's office, but the head teacher sounded more dramatic.

"Well Ruairi does get upset sometimes, doesn't he?"

"Yeah, he does," I said. "Like that time we played snakes and ladders and I won and he tipped the board on the floor."

"Don't let him make you upset," she said.

"I won't." I kicked a pile of leaves and they flew ahead of me in an amber rush.

That weekend, we heard Ruairi's family were moving further north. Up to one of the islands where his cousins lived. "Should we move to the islands?" I asked my dad. He had started to grow a prickly grey beard for no reason he could explain, my mum said he looked like a billy goat.

"It won't make a blind bit of difference," he said. Then, "We're safe here as it is. They're making a song and dance."

The skeleton was displayed in the gym hall with a row of three carved pumpkins. The pumpkins were never lit because we were only in school in daylight hours, but I imagined them lighting themselves at night and turning to grin at each other. The late autumn gales began around that time, I'd sit still and listen to them for long stretches. Some nights the people in tents had to pack up and sleep in their cars and vans. I watched them, warm behind my bedroom window, as they held their hats to their heads, struggled with vehicle doors caught by the wind.

Over the weeks, several other families left for the islands, or arranged to drive south to catch flights to distant countries. Even some of the people in the tents moved further north, including a few new friends I'd hoped to keep. I heard my parents talking from time to time about where we would go if we left, coming back to the fact that we would not go, there was no need.

I bought more items for the dog in hope of the school closing permanently; a tartan collar, a packet of dried treats, a squeaky rubber pheasant.

"Are you going to be getting a pup young lady?" Mr Webster asked at the till.

"Potentially," I said. He laughed and I blushed. I kept all the things I bought in the basket with the pink bone. I resisted buying a coat for the dog because I didn't know what size it would be.

One night in my room after I was supposed to be asleep, I put the light back on and I picked up my favourite book, one about a dog, a cat and a tortoise who go to live on a tropical island. It was full of colourful, detailed illustrations. I opened the first page and held it under the lamp. The familiar, large black type. I stared at it. There was something wrong. I scrunched my eyes then looked at the page again. I couldn't read. Though I could sound out each individual letter, I could not get the words to make sense. It wasn't that they swam in front of my eyes but the opposite, they stayed stuck and stationary on the page. I had been proud of learning to read. In this moment, it seemed to me that I had unlearned. I hurtled myself out of bed and shouted for my parents. My dad came rushing in.

"What is it?"

"I can't read."

"Of course you can read."

"I can't, I can't," I held the book upside down, let it drop onto the floor.

"Shh, you know how to read."

"I forgot."

"People don't forget how to read Elspie." He picked the book up and handed it to me. "It's not the type of thing you can forget." I took it from him and peered at the words on the open page. The words peered back. Glued in their places without meaning.

"I can't read. It's the bomb. It's in my brain," I said, I dropped the book again, arms rigid by my sides.

"Of course it's not. That isn't possible."

"It's brain-damaged me," I said.

My father shook his head. He put the book back on the shelf. "I think it's getting a bit late. This is what happens when children stay up too long."

Eventually, he persuaded me to climb back into bed. I closed my eyes. After the light was put out, fiery alphabets flickered against my eyelids and the quilt became too hot.

The next day I tried not to look at any books or printed words, quickly averting my gaze from any writing I came across. My parents didn't ask me about my lost ability so I didn't mention it.

On Monday when I was back at school, I found I could read my open spelling jotter as normal, scanning it before I even remembered about not being able to read. Everything in the classroom stayed plain and ordinary, except that the clock above the times-table chart seemed to tick far louder than usual so I worked with my head turned away from it.

Over the next few weeks the weather grew colder, we had the first scatterings of snow and bought in a new set of Christmas lights. I collected more rubber bones for the dog. The shop sold dried rawhide chews too but I didn't touch these because they looked like parts of dead things, which after all they were.

We stayed put, we did not want to leave home. As with previous years, I measured winter settling in by the falling of the last leaves from the oak tree that sheltered at the side of our house. Once they were all gone, I sat at the top of the stairs and overheard my parents wondering aloud whether they would ever grow back. Somewhere not so far away, I knew because I'd heard the adults speak of it, there were whole forests where the trees had stopped like broken clocks.

Foday Mannah

Foday Mannah hails from Sierra Leone where he studied English Language and Literature; he then worked as a teacher and lecturer before migrating to the United Kingdom. He lives in Scotland where he is employed as a high school teacher of English. He holds an Msc in International Conflict and Cooperation from the University of Stirling and an MA in Professional Writing from Falmouth University. Foday's writing seeks to represent the experiences of some of the truly remarkable people he has encountered in life. Further inspiration and ideas are provided by his other half Cynthia, and his daughters Tanaka and Mandipa.

Amie Samba

Without warning, Amie Samba the daughter of the local dispenser arrived with Mama Fatu one evening. They walked through us as we played football, the girl crying and carrying her possessions in a weak blue plastic bag. Amie Samba who was svelte and delicate like a mosquito was then made to share a room with Mama Fatu's five daughters. They all lived in a corrugated *pan-body* structure that had been originally painted a pale green, but with time had been invaded by splotches of rust. The house had three bedrooms, wooden windows and no electricity. Standing guard over it was an imposing mango tree that provided shade over an area used for keeping company and braiding hair.

Amie Samba, who was in form three at the Municipal High School at Ferry Junction stopped attending and instead spent her days negotiating chores at Mama Fatu's. These included hand-washing clothes at the nearby stream, filling the big red drum with water and sweeping the wide front yard. Our football games were often punctuated with gossip as to what had caused Amie Samba to live at Mama Fatu's, but even our friend Abdul, Mama Fatu's younger son who slept in the corrugated house at night seemed none the wiser.

With time, we came to conclude that Pa Samba must have had a strong disagreement with his daughter and that Mama Fatu, out of customary magnanimity, had agreed to shelter her. Her father the dispenser was after all a severe man known in the neighbourhood for stiff safari suits, injecting sick adults and circumcising baby boys. Such an association with pain we reasoned logically translated into general cruelty and heartlessness.

Amie Samba's figure however with time helped provide clarity, especially as her daily chores were public performances. The alacrity with which she had carried out her domestic assignments waned, whilst basic movement became more difficult. And since Amie Samba often only wore frayed brassieres and loose *lappas* around her waist, we soon noticed her stomach extending in front of her like a huge polished calabash.

As her stomach continued to grow, Mama Fatu insisted that Amie Samba perform fewer chores, the responsibility of which were passed on to her five daughters. Mama Fatu instead decreed that the child take responsibility for the puppies.

One of the two dogs that lived in Mama Fatu's yard was Morton, a meek mongrel who regularly delivered delightful litters. Morton had one such delivery in the fifth month of Amie Samba's pregnancy.

The dog had chosen to have her offspring in Mama Fatu's outdoor kitchen, a structure constructed of perforated zinc sheets nailed around a rectangular bamboo frame. On the day of Morton's delivery we gathered around Amie Samba in a haphazard phalanx, our eyes bright and eager, listening to her as if to a deity.

Nobody else ventured into the corner of the rusty kitchen where Morton chose to lie, except Amie Samba, whose feet the dog licked. She lifted each squirming creature, peered between its hind legs, before announcing its gender to us younger children who waited at the kitchen door, eyes wide with curiosity.

"This one is a woman," Amie Samba declared before returning the pup to its mother's teat, lifting the next puppy with her free hand in the same movement. "This is also a woman! And she is black and white just like Morton! She's given birth to herself which is always a good sign. One of the babies must always resemble the mother which brings good luck!" After making her way through the litter, she ushered us away so as not to disturb Morton who seemed content and comfortable in an old hi-fi carton, the front side of which had been ripped down and converted into a crude kind of box-bed.

As the puppies' eyes became clearer, Amie Samba would count them every morning in the kitchen where they lay before proceeding to sleep on a rattan mat under the mango tree. The relationship between the dogs and girl was cemented after she boiled a couple of ripe pawpaws and squashed them into an orange paste which she fed to the mother and her offspring. As Morton's teats dried up, Amie Samba would use the crumpled money she kept in her bra to at times buy teaspoons of dried non-fat milk which she would dilute in a dented aluminium bowl. The puppies would slurp up the dull white mixture with gusto, their tails wagging in appreciation. They had by this time graduated from their mother's fastidious attention and instead spent days frolicking around Mama Fatu's yard under the eyes of Amie Samba who would reprimand them with sharp commands if they strayed or transgressed.

Since most of our games flowed in and around Mama Fatu's yard, we continued to interact with Amie Samba, and with time came to realise that she possessed an expansive general knowledge. Her forte was geography and she somehow knew the capital city of every country in the world. A popular game therefore became testing this knowledge, and we would gather around her and her bump like red ants around spilled sugar. She would pause in whatever she was doing, furrow her brow and then supply a response which we would verify in an old coverless school atlas; she never got a single answer wrong. Desperate to see her stumble, we resorted to stretching Amie Samba, taking her away from the comfort of our Africa.

"Honduras," one of us would yell.

"Tegucigalpa," she would reply.

"Peru?"

"Lima."

"How about Qatar?"

"Doha."

"Venezuela?"

"Caracas."

After passing all of our geographical inquisitions, Amie Samba assumed an almost guru-like status and we would come to her with all manner of questions about life and the world we lived in. On afternoons too hot for football, we gathered under Mama Fatu's wide mango tree to play draughts on a faded board. Amie Samba took to playing with us, effortlessly hemming us into positions from which she would eat our pieces.

Dripped gossip eventually revealed the reasons why Mama Fatu had brought Amie Samba to live with her family in the corrugated green house. It was whispered amongst the older ladies who carried water on their heads from the local stream that Tabara, Mama Fatu's older son was responsible for Amie Samba's pregnancy. Tabara's was a nomadic existence, and we were never quite sure if he lived with the rest of the family in the corrugated house. He seemed to spend an endless amount of time in the city and would return on random Sundays wearing white trousers and garish *gara* shirts.

In accordance with native law, Pa Samba had washed his hands of his daughter and claimed that since she was a young school girl who was not married, she could not have climbed into bed with a man let alone be pregnant. In this regard, his final decision was for his daughter to go live with the man who had given her the pregnancy.

But Tabara denied the pregnancy with bulging eyes and claimed that he had never climbed on top of Amie Samba or even seen her underwear. A big palaver followed and Pa Samba burned his daughter's clothes and books before throwing her out of his house. Amie Samba's mother cried and pleaded for her daughter to stay but Pa Samba threatened that she would also leave his house if she dared challenge his decision.

Mama Fatu had therefore said to Pa Samba that because she also had daughters, Amie Samba should come live with her since she had called the name of her son as the owner of the pregnancy. She said that the two families should convene after the baby was born to shake hands and talk over Amie Samba's situation.

By the time Amie Samba gave birth in Mama Fatu's corrugated *pan-body* house on a warm Sunday, all of Morton's puppies except for one female had been distributed through the neighbourhood to bark at thieves in the night. Mama Fatu's son Abdul was with us playing in a cluster of elephant grass that afternoon as he had been thrust away from their house as soon as Amie Samba entered the first throes of labour; Mama Fatu had made him understand that males had no business with sacrosanct female affairs, especially childbirth.

When we returned from school the next day, Mama Fatu's yard had been taken over by a temporary structure constructed out of straight brown sticks covered with palm tree fronds. An assortment of plastic chairs and long benches had been collected from the houses of neighbours and arranged in loose rows beneath the structure.

Our friend Abdul provided us with the details of the previous night, his eyes drawn and tired. Amie Samba had apparently delivered a baby girl after which she had stayed motionless and stiff, thick froth coming out of her mouth. Mama Fatu and the other big women of the area had boiled herbs and said prayers before hurrying to collect Amie Samba's mother. On arrival at Mama Fatu's, she had sunk into the red dust, carried her hands on her head and emitted wrenching sobs which shook her body as if she were suffering the effects of a violent malaria.

A haunted vacant look in his eyes, Abdul continued. "Mama was later able to persuade a taxi driver down at the junction to bring his car over the stones up to the house. Mama and the other women took Amie Samba to Connaught Hospital. They said that she was too weak by the time they got there. The doctors hung a drip on her but unfortunately she did not stay in this world."

The following day, children were kept out of school to show respect, and we sat with the mourners on our best behaviour, listening to whispered conversations. We learned that Pa Samba the dispenser who had disowned his daughter was in the provinces working with Catholic missionaries carrying out immunisation programmes. Mama Fatu's son Tabara had travelled to neighbouring Liberia with a girlfriend who lived in the city and there was talk of him presenting kola nuts to her family as an intention of marriage.

Rice and cassava leaves were cooked in wide pots for the mourners, and we ate in age groups from colourful trays using our hands.

On Friday, Mama Fatu sat on a mat under the mango tree with Amie Samba's mother. Both were attired in grey lace outfits, their eyes bloated and crimson. They stayed at home with a few other relatives and us children whilst most of the area accompanied Amie Samba to the cemetery at Robis. A tall man in a rumpled blue gown read Koranic passages and pointed out that it was never appropriate for a mother to go to the funeral of their child.

After a fortnight, the temporary thatched structure was dismantled, the pillars used as firewood for cooking. Amie Samba's baby daughter, who had been named Zainab, seemed to sleep most of the time in a padded basket under the mango tree, at times opening her eyes to blink at the world around her. Curly hair that looked like strands of black raffia covered her entire head, the front part of which rose and fell in a soft rhythm. She would at times cry, Mama Fatu and her five daughters taking turns to feed and coax her back to satisfied silence.

As Zainab grew, we continued to play in and around Mama Fatu's yard. Added to our games of football and draughts, we took to testing ourselves on the names of capital cities.

Nicholas Petty

Nicholas Petty is a British writer. His story *It is Summer at Camp Pomodoro* was longlisted in the *2019 Sunday Times Audible Short Story Award* and the *2018/19 Galley Beggar Press Short Story Prize*. His work has also been published elsewhere in print and online. He is currently working on a novel. Nicholas grew up in Macclesfield, studied Chemical Engineering at university, and after a stint as a management consultant in London, moved to Utrecht, The Netherlands, where he walks dogs and writes.

These Violent Hands

S he came up with the smoke from the cities. Not fleeing madly like those that came after, but moving away from someone or something.

I first saw her from the valley floor, where I'd spent the day checking empty traps and picking no mushrooms, ignorant of how wrong the world was going. I hiked up the switchbacks to intercept her, dragging in the smoke by the lungful as if I was back at school and trying to fit in. By the time I reached her, she'd plucked up the courage to approach my hut and look through the door.

"Must be one hell of a bonfire," I said.

She spun around. Not quite a rabbit in a hunting lamp. Not quite a cornered boar. She was young, pale, and her eyes were red raw from the stinging air. It was a clammy day but she was wearing a baggy anorak and it was doing a poor job of hiding her pregnant belly.

I repeated myself and smiled, but she gave me a fierce look, probably wondering why I was making jokes given the cities were burning. But I wasn't to know. The news was slow to reach the mountains, slower than the smoke. I never expected things to get so bad and then get worse.

"Who are you?" she asked. A strange question at the time. People came here to forget who they were. To walk and climb and camp and bury the big questions with all the small thoughts these things require.

"I'm Martin and I run this hut," I told her.

"Run it?"

"For the hikers. I'm with the Association."

She gave the hut a doubtful glance. Truth be told it didn't look very official. Like it'd been blown up here from the woods below. There were no signs. I'd been instructed to take them down to make the hut more 'authentic'. Apparently that's what people were missing in their lives back then.

"Do you have any ID?" she asked.

"No ID. You'll have to take my word for it. Now come on, let's get you off your feet."

She gave the hut another once over then made a longer judgement of me. Patched up patches on my knees and elbows. More wrinkles than a map that's been out in the rain and folded wrongly. I've got big strong hands and she watched them for a time.

"I should be on my way," she said, and she walked off up the trail.

It took me a while to come to my senses. Seeing her had surfaced some old memories. Of my ex-wife when she was nearing nine months, and of our own Clare Agnes, born still as a mountain lake.

"You should stay here tonight. It's dangerous in the dark," I called after her.

"I'll be fine on my own," she called back.

"You might fall."

"I can manage."

There was only one thing I knew that would bring her round. Folks will go scrambling up loose rocks that'd crush them faster than they can say avalanche, but threaten them with lightning and they'll squirm into the hut three to a bed. So I said, "There'll be a storm tonight."

She stopped to look up at the sky. "You sure?"

"Certain," I lied. The sky was grey but calm and there was no indication the weather would foul, but in fairness to me it had been all over the place recently.

"I don't have any money," she said.

"Nor do I."

"I mean to pay you. For the lodging."

"I know, I'll keep it off the books." I winked and tapped my nose, a stupid gesture that made her flinch. But then she looked up at the sky again, imagining the shock of a million volts through her unborn child, no doubt.

"What's your name?" I asked.

She blinked as though she'd near enough forgotten. "I'm Sophie. Sophie Parton."

The hut felt smaller on the inside and the air was heavy, salty. Smelt of smoke, but wood smoke, not that bitter stuff that came up from the cities. There was a stove, a table, and some long benches. The benches doubled up as beds, one of which was mine, and a ladder led up to a low attic where a few more can stay. Slept eight uncomfortably and sixteen very uncomfortably.

I gave Sophie Parton some water. She took it like she hadn't drunk for days. Then I started up the wood burner. It was tinned soup for dinner. The Association used to deliver the supplies by mule and charged the hikers an arm and a leg and then another arm. But I didn't charge Sophie Parton and that seemed to scare her some more.

We stayed sitting at the table after dinner. I hoped more people would arrive and settle her down. A couple of women or a young family. But it was mid-week, end-of-season, and as it turned out the world was ending so no one came by. I asked her some questions about herself to show I meant no harm. She told me she worked in a laundrette and the lady in charge made her feel worthless and ashamed and full of hate. She didn't mention a partner or anything.

When it got darker I lit a couple of oil lamps. Then I saw it, the swelling on Sophie Parton's left cheek, shining and shadowed in the uplight. Can't imagine she'd walked into a door but I didn't say anything. Not my business.

She looked exhausted, but she didn't want to drop off before she'd sussed me out properly. So she started her interrogating.

"Where are you from?" she asked.

"Not far from here. Was born in a town in the foothills."

"Do you have a family?"

She wanted me to tell her stories of children and grandchildren, but I disappointed. "I don't. An ex-wife."

"What happened?" Her eyes moved to my big hands again.

I didn't want to talk about our Clare Agnes. About how cold she'd been when we'd dressed her that one time. How that cold had spread through the house and how her silence had drowned out our talking.

"When something bad happens you might want to run in opposite directions. I wanted to go up, she wanted to go down. Me to the mountains, her to the city. Simple as that."

"She's in the city now?"

"Heard she's got a husband. Estate agent. Successful."

"It's not safe in the cities," she said, and there was some blame in her voice.

"It's never been safe," I said.

"It's getting worse. People are on the streets most nights. Burning stuff."

"As if it isn't warm enough already," I joked, but she wasn't laughing.

"Trees, cars, buildings. A pile of books as big as a house."

I didn't want to get dramatic so I said, "I'm sure someone will sort it all out eventually."

She touched the swelling on her face, her mind off imagining some swinging fist, no doubt. "But who?"

I busied myself with the fire. Sawed up a couple of big logs I'd misjudged in the chopping and couldn't fit through the stove door. I keep a large hacksaw in the hut for such things. She watched me the whole time. Watched my big hands on the saw, the blade in the wood. I tried to make her loosen up if only so I could.

"You okay there, Sophie Parton?" I asked.

She didn't respond. I stopped and hung up the hacksaw. She watched it all the way onto the nail.

"I'd appreciate it if you relax a little," I said.

"You told me there was going to be a storm."

Sophie Parton refused to sleep in the attic and instead sat awake by the door. I read for a bit before snoozing off. The last thing I saw was her looking out the window, waiting for the flash of lightning that would justify her decision to bunk in with me.

I dreamt of rabbit and mushroom stew probably. Not like the dreams I have these days. And I woke up to find Sophie Parton standing over me.

She'd undone her coat and her belly poked out from beneath her t-shirt. She seemed so fragile, like a broken pot that's been balanced back together without any glue, and I was afraid I might cause complications just by moving. But there was a tension in her too, like a freshly primed trap.

"Couldn't sleep?" I asked.

"You said there would be a storm." Her voice was louder than it had been before.

"It might storm. It might not. Difficult to tell these days."

"But you said you were *certain*."

I tried to sit up and she kind of lunged forward so I settled back down all slowly.

"You lied to get me in here, didn't you?" she said.

"It's okay, Sophie Parton, you're safe with me."

"That's what they all say."

It was then that I saw the hacksaw was missing from the nail, and that it was in Sophie Parton's delicate right hand. I reckoned what I said next was important for my own health so I chose my words as best I could. "I'm not going to hurt you, Sophie Parton. You can trust me."

Her shoulders slumped and she sighed, and I thought that maybe she'd come round. But I realise now she wasn't coming to terms with my words, but with what she was about to do.

Back went the saw and then down. She hit me just above the knee, a fleshy bit thankfully. I was wearing my lumbering trousers so it didn't break the skin, just pranged off and left a few toothy bruises. Then she raised the saw above her head. Turned it sideways.

I try to tell myself I would have let it happen. That I knew none of this was her fault. That I would have let her saw off my whole head slowly if it meant not harming her or her baby.

A flash of lightning. Thunder. Then again. Brighter. Louder.

Sophie Parton stepped back and her killing arm dropped to her side, a turmoil thrashing through her like trees in the wind. That I hadn't lied, though I had, albeit whitely. And that she was a killer, though she wasn't, albeit she had potential. Another flash, more thunder, a noise so deep it rolled around my gut, hummed to the ends of the arms. Though maybe that wasn't just the storm outside, maybe that was the storm in me.

Because this is what really gets to me. After all that, she took one look at me and turned on her heels, decided to brave the lightning instead of me, crashing out the door with her belly in one hand and the saw in the other. I can only think I must have had some mean, mean manner about me.

When I'd calmed down I stood at the entrance to the hut. Watched the storm cross over the valley until everything stilled. The clattering pines turned quiet. The smoke cleared. A sliver of moon crawling across the sky. The cloddy smell of fallen rain and the thirsty ground drinking up the last puddles we've had for some time.

I didn't find Sophie Parton's burnt out corpse on the path so I assume the lightning left her alone. She must have come across other huts like mine further down the trail. I hope she didn't take shelter. The mountains and the weather are dangerous but they aren't cruel. But who knows what I could have been.

I certainly don't. Not any more. Because most nights I dream of her aiming that saw at my neck and the storm doesn't come and I'm not so accepting. I'm up on my feet and I'm fighting and there's blood so much blood.

I often think of holding Clare Agnes for the last time, her skin as smooth as a cool pebble. She was so small she could near enough lie flat across my palm. Though the mountains have trenched a few scars into my hands since, they've never felt rougher and clumsier than they did then. I loved her and I was terrified, as though my big hand might suddenly ball into a horrible fist.

And that's all I can think of now. Not her perfect fingers, her perfect nose, her perfect feet. But of my violent hands, and the violent hands of others.

Carina Swantee

Carina Swantee has studied Art, Photography and Creative Writing in London. Carina grew up in Sweden and moved abroad in her twenties. She is a Faber Academy Alumna and a member of *Chrysalis Writing Group* in Richmond. In 2015, she was published in *Fusion*, the anthology of The Complete Creative Writing Course, and she was longlisted for the Bristol Short Story Prize in 2017. She speaks five languages and lives in Zurich with her husband, their three kids and their flat-coated retriever. She is currently editing her first novel, *The Silver Barn*.

The Farmhand

1

Midsummer

Sometimes Farmer Anderson could get rather repetitive, Sven thought, and took another spoonful of the potato soup. His current theme was the advantages of the new tractor, and the farmer had got all wound up about it. His voice rose and fell as in a song, and sometimes he burst out in laughter, in a way people do, when they seldom meet other people.

Sven knew a thing or two about tractors, even though his father had worked the fields the hard and traditional way, with horses. They were sold at auction many years ago, along with the other cattle, the farm and all the land, to pay his father's debts. Farmer Anderson's farm was well-kept and tidy. His father's farm had been everything else but that, especially at the end. But Sven knew a lot about engines. He could pluck an engine apart, oil every piece of it, assemble it again and it would work like clockwork.

Sitting on the hard bench under the window at the wooden kitchen table, absently chewing the bread, Sven nodded his head in reply when there was a slight pause, while his thoughts wandered elsewhere – for example, towards Rachel, the farmer's sister, who sat at the other end of the table. Her face wasn't very pretty. It was meagre, lined and weathered and her freckled nose was strong and sharp. But when Rachel occasionally stood up, to get one thing or the other from the kitchen counter, he felt an inner joy watching her. The simple cotton dress couldn't hide those legs, so tall, so strong, reaching all the way up to the thin waist. The fabric was thinned by age and harsh sunshine, bleached into a mild yellow tone, and the blue flowers were hardly distinguishable any more. She had pulled her silvery hair back into a bun on top of her head and it bounced and shimmered in the light that entered through the windowpane.

Farmer Anderson continued talking with a monotone voice about the crop, hands wearily scratching his raspy cheeks. Still watching Rachel, Sven was considering sharing some of the things he knew about crops. She in turn looked out of the window, her blue watery eyes gazing towards the silo on the other side of the yard, which was bathed in late afternoon sunlight. A heavy wooden ladder was propped against the windowless wall with a stained bucket of paint hooked onto one of the steps. After a week on the farm Sven had painted a bit more than half of the faded building in a dark red. Furthermore, Anderson wished the large doors and the window frames to be painted black. All in all, he had promised Sven two weeks of lodging and food over the agreed pay.

'Huh?' Sven asked, suddenly aware of the silence around the table and their questioning looks.

'Rachel,' Farmer Anderson said and nodded towards his sister.

'What about her?' Sven asked, his cheeks blushing. Confused he reached for another piece of flat bread and spread some butter on it.

'You ought to take her out for a ride on that motorcycle of yours.' Anderson rose with difficulty and limped over the wooden floorboards to the range, put another log into the fire and filled his mug with coffee. 'It's the longest day of the year,' he said and took a cautious sip of the coffee. 'So, why don't you two drive around a little?'

Farmer Anderson was probably ten or even fifteen years his senior. A scar, shimmering white, lined his chin. That and the limp made him look old. His trousers were baggy and worn, clinging on to his meagre body with the help of a pair of braces.

'I could also finish the west side tonight,' Sven said hesitantly. 'Could start fresh tomorrow with the north side.'

'Rachel, it'd do you some good.' Farmer Anderson was interrupted by a wheezing cough.

'No,' she said, pressing her thin lips tight. It was the first thing she'd said during the entire meal.

'You can take some petrol from the barn,' Farmer Anderson said.

'I should clean my brushes.' Sven stood up and thanked them politely for the supper. He wiped his mouth on the worn napkin and left it on the table, neatly folded.

Farmer Anderson got his way and a little later, protected from the wind and potential falls by helmets and goggles, Sven and Rachel were driving through the countryside on his motorbike.

'You all right?' he called out, shifting the gear with his boot.

She shouted something back, but he couldn't hear what, just felt the warm breath in his neck and the vibration of her voice against his back.

The wheat fields lining the roads were green-gleaming, sprouting light-heartedly, and the engine of the Triumph Bonneville puttered and purred underneath them as Sven steered the machine carefully over the gravel road. Rachel's arms embraced Sven's waist, not too hard and not too soft. Her hands were determinately placed against his belly and chest, he could feel the warmth of the palms of her hands through his linen shirt.

He slowed down and she came up closer, and they leant harmoniously in the curves.

The next evening, neither of them really minded as Farmer Anderson made them go on a tour with the motorcycle again. They made a stop down at the waterside and he parked the motorbike next to a juniper bush. The farmer's sister took off her helmet and shook her head and her silvery hair rolled down her back. She stood in front of him, her features softened by the warm evening light, and he approved of that she was as tall as himself. But how old she could be? Five? Or even ten years older than himself?

He followed her on the path towards the boulders lining the bay. They sat down on a rock, which was still generating heat from the day's sunrays. Its surface was soft like velvet. They watched the heifers wading in the shallow water on the other side of the bay and he searched his familiar, unspoken restlessness within, but couldn't find it. The restlessness that drove him on and on, North and South, West and East, was nowhere to be found. He was calm inside, watching the rowing boat slowly gliding randomly over the water, while the fisherman threw his flies over the glimmering surface.

Her hair spread out on the boulder as she lay down on her back and he bent over her, whispered with his mouth close to hers, what he needed to know, 'How old are you?'

'Old enough,' she replied.

Her mouth tasted of warm milk, honey and fresh-baked bread.

'And how old are you?'

'Old enough,' he mumbled in reply.

Autumn arrived, colouring the countryside red, yellow and orange and by the time they got married in the village church, Sven had painted everything. Both the barn and the silo in deep red, with black doors and gates. The farmhouse shone white like a mansion. He had even painted the wooden fence surrounding the garden.

In church, Rachel wore a short white dress. Accompanied by her brother she walked towards him up the aisle, her long hand resting on Farmer Anderson's arm. With a pillbox hat placed on her silvery hair she looked like she'd just stepped out from a fashion magazine. Sven straightened as he watched her shape moving in a beam of sunlight entering through the stained-glass windows, slightly distorted from the tears rising in his eyes, feeling deeply grateful for the new suit that Farmer Anderson had insisted on buying him.

The morning after their celebration, as Sven was about to hang the suit back into the cupboard in their new room, the birdsong from the window suddenly mixed with the sound Farmer Anderson's wheezing coughing and of Rachel calling out in desperation. He tumbled down the stairs and out on the yard, towards his newly wedded wife. Rachel was kneeling by her brother, a lifeless heap of blue overalls in the middle of the yard, crying silently with trembling shoulders. Anderson opened his eyes and gave him a last glance, before he slowly closed his eyes again.

For Sven, this would always remain the decisive moment, when Farmer Anderson wordlessly handed over his sister Rachel to him, to Sven, for eternity.

2
Christmas

It was the shortest day of the year. Rachel moved in behind the lace curtain, lifted the latch again and opened the window. Fresh air swept in and she listened for the sound of the tractor. Sven should be back from North Forest by now. She could hear no other sound but the black crow, sending its cryptic message over the village. Shuddering, she wrapped the scarf tighter around the shoulders. The wind from the sea was cold. She could smell the snow in the air. The brown fields would soon be powdered white.

She looked out over the tidy yard. Machines and tools in their places. Their buildings newly painted. They had never paid the temporary farmhand, but look what he'd got instead. Look what she'd got. Although she was worried, a little smile lingered on her lips as she closed the window again. She couldn't really grasp that she was the mistress of the farm now, it was hers and she was married. Her brother was gone and with him his illness, his darkness. She folded her hands and sent him a silent thank you. It had taken her some time to accept her brother's intentions. It was the unintentional intimacy on that motorbike that had given her an inkling, a taste of the possibility of another future.

Exchanging silent and expectant looks during the hectic preparations, she and Sven were ready now for the coming of winter; its short days with only a few hours of daylight at the darkest time of the year. They had stocked hay for the animals in the barn, the hens and the cows were secured and warm in their stalls in the cowshed. Vegetables, berries and fruits were conserved in glasses or dried in baskets, the fish and meat salted.

On the way back to the kitchen, she stopped at the looking glass in the hallway, lifted a hand and arranged her plaited hair on her neck. Her face was the same, but there was a light in her eyes. But her smile faded as she saw the touch of sunset in the reflection, and a shiver wandered down her spine when the clock started to strike. One, two, three… Her stomach churned.

It was getting late. Way too late.

She hurried back to the kitchen, where she shoved the saucepan with the potatoes away from the heat. She put a lid over the stew, which puttered on the range in the coolest zone. Then she went back to the hallway and sat down on a stool, her lips moving wordlessly and her hands trembling as she pulled another pair of socks over her feet and laced her boots. She pulled a bonnet over her head and grabbed a coat from the hook. Quickly she ran out through the door and down the steps.

Dusk. Her feeling of urgency grew. Soon it would be dark. She ran over the yard, sliding over the frozen soil, and took her bicycle from the stable wall. She sat up and turned the pedals, kicking the light on with the tip of her boot.

Rachel cycled down the driveway, out on the big road. The wind bit her cheeks and she pulled the bonnet further down over her ears. On the way to the North Forest she passed the last house in the village, wondering for a moment if she should ask them for help. Through the window, she could see the family gathered around the kitchen table. But she didn't want to waste any more time, it would take too long to explain. She cycled harder and as she entered the forest, the road became bumpy and unfriendly. She navigated the bicycle around treacherous branches and deep holes. This road was difficult to ride on even in summertime. After a while she could see the fresh trail from a tractor disappearing in among the trees on her left and jumped off the bicycle, let it lean onto to a juniper bush by the verge. She stood still, trying to get her panting breath under control and listened. 'Sven,' she called out in the wind. 'Where are you?'

A crow screeched.

She ventured further into the trees, the long dead grass grasped after her ankles, trying to snare her, make her fall.

'Sven!' Her voice echoed in the stillness. She listened.

Just when she was about to start moving again, she could hear a muffled voice calling and hurried towards it, stumbled over a fallen tree trunk, searching with her eyes until she could see something red glimpsing behind the trees. The tractor.

'Sven?' Her voice was filled again with determination. It came from the anger she felt with herself, standing by the window, hovering and daydreaming in front of the looking glass, while her husband was hurt, trapped somewhere.

'I'm here!'

She rushed around the tractor and there he was. Sven lay on his side, his arms free, but his lower body was trapped under the trunk of a big pine.

'Oh Sven,' Rachel mumbled, falling to the ground. 'Are you all right?' She pulled off her scarf and put it under his head, lifting it carefully from the branches covering the ground, while adjusting his cap. She pulled off her mittens and cupped his shivering cheeks.

Sven was pale, but he smiled weakly. 'It's not so bad, just bloody cold. Can you move the tree?'

'Sure.' She smiled confidently and stood up, put both her hands on the trunk and tried to push it away from him. The resistant bark scratched her bare hands and the tree didn't move an inch.

'It's too heavy,' Sven said.

'Wait,' she commanded, and turned back to the tractor. She climbed into the cab, tucked the sheepskin from the seat under her arm and searched feverishly until she found the heavy chain in a metal box.

It scrambled and clinked over the ground as she hurried back and started to latch it around the trunk. She took a big step over him and with fingers aching from the cold, she managed to hook the other end of the chain onto the back of the tractor.

'I'll build a protection, so that the tree can't fall back on you,' she said, trying to tuck the sheepskin around his chest. Then she collected loose branches and built a fence around him. The fragile trunks were arranged in such a way, that when the tree started to move, it would slide over the wood without hurting him.

'I have it, I can push it if you move it,' Sven mumbled, gripping his arms around the trunk.

'We'll do this together. You will be just fine.' She rushed back to the tractor and sat up on the iron seat. Shivering from cold and fear she turned the key, pressing the accelerator with her foot. The engine started with a roar. 'Ready?' she called out.

It was difficult to move the stick into first gear, but Rachel knew that already and took her time, using both hands. Black smoke rose from the exhaust pipe as she took a deep breath, gripped the wheel as her trembling foot gently lifted the clutch, urging the tractor to move forwards. The colossal wheels creaked and the rolled-up chain rattled behind her and she could feel the resistance as it started to stretch. Finally, she could hear the tree trunk crackling. 'Slowly, slowly,' she mumbled through gritted teeth.

'It's fine, keep going.' Sven's voice had regained its force.

She turned, watched the trunk move inch by inch and she held her breath.

It's fine it's fine. Keep going keep going.

After a few metres, she shoved the gear back in neutral, pulled the handbrake and jumped down. Behind the tractor, Sven had rolled over, trying to stand on all four. His eyes shone black in his face, which was as white as the fog surrounding them. He tempted a grin before he closed his eyes and sacked down on the ground.

She kneeled next to him and tried to move him. But his body was slack and unwilling. She gave up and slumped down in the rustling frozen grass next to him, panting. 'Sven?' she whispered. There was no answer but the whistling wind. She closed her eyes. The smell of snow mixed with the scent of sweet water rising from the whipping waves in the bay behind the pines. Wasn't this her destiny? she wondered. Had she really thought that she could escape this hopeless loneliness?

A sudden flicker deep in her belly startled her and instinctively her hand moved there, briefly cupping the wool of her skirt. She smiled weakly and waited. There was no more. She took a deep breath and turned to her husband, tried turning him over on his side. She let out a strained sob while examining his body, her hands patting over his thick overalls. There was no blood anywhere, but his left leg was strangely twisted and when she took a firm hold of it to turn it with the rest of the body, his eyelids fluttered and he let out a pained groan.

'You're fine,' she said, rubbing his shoulders with her hands, patting his arms. The energy was back in his body.

'I am?' he asked.

'Yes, sit up.' She stood up and smiled, gently brushing some pine needles from his cheek with the palm of her hand. 'Come on.'

'I can't.' He shook his head and prodded his finger to the twisted leg.

'It's broken.' Rachel took his hands and pulled him up in a sitting position. Then she took off her coat and wrapped it around him, helped him to his feet. 'Could have been worse,' she said, tucking his arm over her shoulder. His body leaned heavily on hers and with an arm slung around his waist, she slowly led him to the tractor.

Well there, Sven stared at the door, which was still swung open, and the two insurmountable steps leading up to the cab. 'Can't do that,' he grunted. 'Never.'

'Hold on,' she said and climbed into the cab. Sitting down on the other side of the seat she leant out towards him and grabbed his wrists, and inch by inch, Rachel lifted Sven into the tractor, spurred on by the pain of the edges of the seat cutting into her chest. 'We can do this,' she mumbled through gritted teeth, to her husband, to the little fish that had flicked deep down in her belly.

With the help of his arms and his unharmed leg, Sven slowly turned and took a seat on the window frame beside her, letting out a loud groan of pain and relief. She rose to place a quick kiss on his sweaty brow before she took the driver's seat, started the engine anew and slowly steered them back to the gravel road, snowflakes whirling in the headlights.

Two days later, in the wake of Christmas Eve and with the help from the neighbours down the road, their tree was finally placed in the kitchen. Rachel had never seen a thicker or more perfect tree. They decorated it together with red Christmas baubles, but only after Sven had drilled little holes in the trunk and filled in the additional branches that he had been collecting in the forest.

In the flickering candle light, she played Silent Night on the piano, patiently expecting another sign from the little wonder sheltered in her belly, and she watched over Sven, who lay propped up on pillows and plaids on the bench beneath the window. He had a cast on his wounded leg and could make himself about the house with the help of a pair of wooden crutches. The next time the sensation was there, she would tell him.

Outside the landscape rested, silently waiting under a thick coat of snow.

Sophie Tiefenbacher

Sophie Tiefenbacher was born in a small town in Austria and now lives in Cambridge where she works as a writer and editor. Bilingual in German and English, she completed a degree in Comparative Literature at the University of Vienna before winning a scholarship to read Creative Writing at the University of Oxford.

Tiger Meat

I t rained every day. Water dripped through the cracks in the ceiling and seeped in under the doors. In the carpets, big patches of mould grew like flowers. We took to sleeping under tarps that collected pools overnight.

Sandra kept saying that it was temporary, that we were getting back on our feet. But in the evenings, when she sat at the kitchen table smoking with Nick, his hand creeping higher and higher up her thigh while the water dripped into salad bowls and casserole dishes, it fell to me to put the little ones to bed, and I knew that she would sit there, smoking, until the morning. She had not learned from the past. I lay awake, listening to the rain gurgling in the gutters like a stomach ache.

Nick kept us fed. It was always turkey. The soil was black from the rain and full of stones, the turkeys turning them over with their claws and uprooting anything that came up. They were sickly birds, skin drawn tight between claws, their beady eyes unblinking. None of them lived long, their feathers growing thin and brittle and their sagging necks quivering as they watched us through the fence. Nick killed them himself. He put on his plastic apron, slick with rain, and carried the birds to the barn by their legs, unbothered by their flapping and screaming. I sat between the rusted motorcycles and the old furniture and watched him swing his axe.

They know what's coming, Nick said, cupping my ass as he walked by. The fear goes into the meat, makes it tender.

I kept quiet.

We made stew out of the meat, sausages with slivers of winter-soft apples, meat pies, broth from the bones. The little ones turned the feathers into necklaces that smelled of death in the rain.

We ate turkey until we could not taste it anymore, the meat bloating in our mouths as if we were chewing our own tongues.

It's temporary, Sandra said. At least you're not going hungry.

When his associates came over, Nick did the cooking, a cigarette wedged into his teeth as he flipped meat in the pan. Sandra served drinks the same colour as the rain water in the salad bowls. They were entrepreneurs, talking business and product in guffawing voices that woke the little ones until I had to chase after them and jiggle them back to sleep on my knee, their feet leaving muddy prints down my sides.

There were packages wrapped in plastic that changed hands at the kitchen table, large wooden crates that left a trail of soggy wood shavings on the carpet, and yellow envelopes of the kind that were padded with bubble wrap. I didn't ask what was inside.

A man with a business mind can go far in the world, Nick told me as we were taking the leftovers out back to the turkeys, tossing them the bones of their siblings through the fence, eager beaks clicking.

The rain fell in sheets. I could not remember the sun. Nick took a step closer, his cigarette still glowing despite the rain. He pressed into me, the wood of the barn door damp against my back, the turkeys gurgling, choking on their own gristle. He said my name, and I sucked in a mouthful of rain, twisted out of his grip, and ran. At night, I lay awake, thinking I could feel my bones rot.

One day before dinner, Nick made a big show out of leading us out to the barn, through the turkey coop. The turkeys were digging in the mud, their red skin rimmed with white, like mould had taken root, flocking away from our boots in pressed silence as if they knew what sat behind the barn door.

Nick let us peek one by one, opening the door just an inch, holding the little ones' hands and hugging Sandra round the waist when it was her turn. She let out a laugh and pushed back into him.

Have you gone mad, she said, staring into the darkness behind the door, her voice quivering with delight.

Can we keep him? the little ones begged, their fingernails digging into my hands.

I stepped closer, blinking, the smell of wet soil filling my nose, and underneath it, animal.

The tiger's claws clicked softly as it paced the barn, its tail swishing and its eyes tracking us. Its stripes melted into the darkness, emerging again in unexpected places, ghostlike and fast. My skin crawled.

Isn't she a beauty, Nick said, his hand cupping me hidden behind the door, where Sandra couldn't see. His breath fell hot against my ear, and then he pushed the door shut, the bolt falling heavily into place.

Don't get too attached, he said. She'll be gone by tomorrow.

That night, I lay awake, the crinkling of tarps and dripping of water making my insides turn. I didn't bother putting on shoes when I went back out to the barn, mud clinging to my hem and catching between my toes. The turkeys rustled their feathers as I walked past, blinking night-blind into the darkness, the rain glinting off their bald patches.

The tiger was pacing the barn, the air heavy with the scent of something big in a space too small. I held my breath and stood very still, my hands on the door. The tiger kept moving, but its ears turned in my direction, muscles rolling under the fur.

She pretends she doesn't care, Nick said, sliding out of the shadows behind me. But I know better.

I held on to the barn door, my knuckles pressing through my skin. Rain water was rising in my throat.

Imagine how she would taste, Nick said, all that tender meat.

He licked my neck, just underneath my ear, his tongue cold and slick.

When we got up in the morning, the turkey coop was empty. Blood pooled between pebbles in the mud, wet feathers in clumps, claws pointing skyward. The little ones dug a beak out of the earth. The barn door stood ajar.

Sandra combed through the empty rooms of the house, turning out damp drapes and rugs, calling for Nick. I stood outside, listening to the rain.

Liz Tresidder

Liz Tresidder is a young writer based in the South West. Whilst studying film at university, she found herself drawn to the portrayal of women's relationships with the domestic and natural spaces, a theme which now frequently appears in her writing. *from the forest* is her first piece of published work.

from the forest

'It's not fair to leave it like that.'

'I know.'

The gun is heavy slung over her shoulder like this. Awkwardly, she shrugs, readjusts her hold so the metal doesn't bite into her skin so much.

'Shoot it.'

Greg stuffs his hands into the pockets of his jacket. It's the windbreaker that she'd gotten him for Christmas last year; smart, with an insulated lining. It rustles, now, as he buries his nose further into his scarf and looks at her from under his brows. She studies the little bit of his face left behind.

'What?' He asks, shrugging. 'It'll bleed out.'

'Greg –'

'It'll just be in pain. For hours. Is that what you would want?'

She tilts her head, considering. The leg is maimed, but the wound to the stomach isn't bad enough to kill it quickly. Greg's right; a slow, drawn out death. Still –

'Do you want me to do it?' He asks, palm outstretched. The gun presses down further into her shoulder.

He always did have strange hands. Pale, the underside so white she can see the veins in the fleshy pad by his thumb. But the tops of his fingers are cracked and red with eczema, so that holding his hand gives the odd sensation of cupping an orange cut in two. The warmth and silky wetness of the flesh giving way to a hard, pitted skin. Often, late at night, she'll wake to him scratching in his sleep. In the morning the skin in the webs of his fingers will have caramelised to a flaky wetness, sticky to the touch.

She pushes the gun off her shoulder and lets it dangle loosely from her hand for a moment. It knocks against her calf and she wavers her head from side to side, deciding.

'No. It's alright. You go to the car, turn the heating on. I'll be there in a minute.'

He turns his hand all the way over, palm towards the sky now, as if hiding the redness of his knuckles from her. She wishes he would wear gloves. She passes him the car keys and watches him trudge away.

It's that nice time of day, where the sun is just beginning to set and hangs low in the sky. The air around her is spilled full of gold, and with all the trees beginning to turn it's as if the entire forest is on fire.

There's blood on her jeans.

'Shit.' She crouches down to consider the stain, licking at her thumb and swiping at it – but no. It's engrained in the denim now.

'*Please.*'

Soap and warm water. She'll do it as soon as she's home.

She'd been surprised she'd made the shot, to be honest. She'd been aiming for the head – but he had been fast, hunkered down low, and so she'd just knicked the soft underbelly instead. It'd barely slowed him down. The trap had caught him in the end.

Nasty way to go.

'*Please.*'

Second time he's said that now. Slowly, she straightens, pulls the gun up and begins to load the bullets. It clicks, quietly, with each mechanism pulled apart and reset.

He'd looked strong – that's why she'd been surprised. She'd wanted to go for something easier but Greg had insisted, had pressed the gun into her hands and told her to breathe. *In. Out. Take your time. Line up the shot. He can't hear us – we're too far away.*

'I don't –' he pauses, takes a moment to roll over, hand cradling his stomach, and cough. Blood dribbles against his chin. 'I don't wanna die – hey –'

'Listen –' he hears her cock the gun and begins to wriggle, dragging himself hand over hand through the leaves. The trap on the leg pulls him short. She watches the body turn concave, bent like a comma.

Sighing, she slings the gun back over her shoulder and crouches down. Puts a hand on his jaw and waits until his eyes meet hers. Blood and saliva drips through the lines of her palm. 'You've been shot in the stomach. Not bad, just a graze, but what with the leg wound as well you'll bleed out. If you're lucky. If not, you'll have to wait for infection. Could take days.' She tries to mediate her voice into something soothing. 'Wouldn't you rather I just shot you now?'

He rolls his head to one side and coughs out a mouthful of blood.

'Take me to a hospital,' he grinds out, dragging his knee upwards through the leaves. She's never seen something move like that before; the wriggling of a worm slowed down to half-speed, the whole body curving and retracting and winding up again with pain.

'It'll be quick,' she informs him as she straightens up. The cold wet of the ground has seeped through the knees of her jeans and she swipes at them absently.

'That man,' he starts up, but his voice catches, the second word cracking in half. *Ma-an.* He clears his throat, a suckling sound of liquid in his windpipe, and starts again. 'That man. He your boyfriend?'

She shakes her head.

'Husband.'

On an instinctive recoil, the image of Greg flashes up in her mind. Tall and skinny, like a rake. It was how he'd caught her attention from across the room, at the party where they'd first met. He'd towered half a head above everyone else, so tall his hair had brushed against the lamp shade when he'd followed her into the kitchen to introduce himself.

He nods, raises a slow hand and swipes blood from his chin. His lips have turned blue. He must be cold; the skin along his arms is goose pimpled, the dark, fine hair raised up away from his skin. The forest around them swells with quiet and she realises she can hear his teeth chattering.

'I had a girl. While back.' Slowly, every movement wading through the treacly pools of golden hour sunlight, he turns over until his shoulder blades meet the forest floor. 'Will you do me a favour?'

When she doesn't say anything, he slides his gaze until it reaches her. She nods.

'In my front pocket, there's a picture.'

They put the body in the boot of the car.

'Pasta for dinner?' Greg asks her as they sit in the traffic, late-afternoon radio a buzz in the background.

'Sure.'

Greg nods, switches lanes and clucks his tongue irritably as someone cuts him off and he has to tap the breaks, lurching them both forward in their seats slightly.

She forgets about the photo until she's sorting laundry. Her clothes have mingled with Greg's, so that she ends up separating his socks from her pants. They cling together with static and she gets a soft, furry sort of shock when she makes contact with them.

She's folding when the photo falls out onto her lap. Her jeans still have little droplets of blood on the cuff and she's momentarily distracted, scraping at the stain with her thumbnail, until the photograph topples from her knee to the floor. The sound of it against their worn lino – a soft tap, like when you start flicking through pages in a book – catches her short and she stops. Places the jeans down carefully. Picks up the photograph.

'She was beautiful,' the man tells her. He's pushed up on his elbows, eyes flickering across the photograph she's holding. Back and forth, like a light bulb just starting to dim. Buzzing in and out. She's surprised, then, when his gaze shoots up to her and she finds herself studying the photograph too. The intensity in his eyes, the clearness where moments ago they had been clouded in a way she's seen so many times before – in deer and rabbits and foxes and people, caught in traps, waiting to bleed out – shocks her.

He was right. The woman was beautiful. The person behind the camera had caught her off guard; she's strung halfway between a hard look and a smile, gazing over her shoulder. A cloud of blonde hair softens the sharp jaw, the thin purse of the lips sliding into a grin. The photo is in black and white but she can tell her eyes were pale; grey, maybe, or blue.

It's soft, now. The photograph. A crease runs across her face, little flecks of the photo paper pulled away from a turn in the washer so that her nose is interrupted by a thin white line. The corners, which had been so sharp before – as if he'd just had the photo printed yesterday – have been rounded out and when she pushes against them they bend to the pads of her fingers.

'We got married last year.' He holds up his hand, shows her his ring finger. A simple band; silver, rather than gold. Unusual.

Her own rings glint in the low sun coming in through the window. Greg had gotten Coldplay lyrics engraved into their wedding bands.

'How long?' He asks, nodding towards her hand. She curls her fingers protectively over the ring.

'Three months.'

'Newlyweds.'

He had said it knowingly, a wry grin on his face, the lift of his mouth slightly distorted by the smear of blood running across his jaw. If she looked at him too quickly it was as if his smile stretched all the way up to his ear.

He nods, finally. Lays back and holds his hand out.

His fingers are freezing and for a moment she thinks he's going to drop the photograph in the leaves. But he doesn't. Instead, he grips a little harder, so that the paper bends slightly, and he rustles amongst the forest floor as he lifts his hand. Studies the photo a last time.

She feels an odd lurch in her stomach as she studies it now, the blonde girl with the big blue eyes and the whip-smart smile. He had kept the photograph in the breast pocket of his jacket. It had still been warm with the heat from his chest when she'd handled it, back in the forest.

'Alright,' he tells her, nodding. He slips the photo between his fingers and rests his hand on his sternum. The paper quivers ever so slightly with the shake of his hands. 'Alright,' he repeats, and lays his head all the way down.

That night, Greg slides into bed and kisses her neck. When his hand wraps round her bare shoulder, slipping under her bra strap, a wetness gels with her skin and when he pulls away he sticks, ever so slightly, to her. The sore of eczema where he had been scratching at the dinner table, tacky and damp. In the morning it will have crystalised once again, hard flakes of skin and pus buried in the webs of his hands.

Sean Watkin

Sean Watkin is a Creative Writing graduate from Liverpool John Moores and is studying for a Masters in Writing. Sean is working hard on his first novel whilst studying and working full time as a Communications Officer. He has edited and published two e-zines, and has hosted writing events for the LGBT+ community. When taking breaks from writing his novel, he writes short stories and articles, having published the series *Dating Sean* for Seen Magazine Liverpool, *Am I a Survivor Yet?* and *A Journey to Orlando* for The Gay UK, and *PTSD and How it Affects You* for The Content Wolf.

I Walked There

I walked there. It was six miles and to me then it seemed like nothing; like a walk anyone would do for someone who was interested in them. It was a walk Buffy would do for Angel. The sunken arches of my feed throbbed, and November howled over bald fields empty of animals and crops. The season's rake fingers almost tore through the cream-coloured fleece Nan had given to me. I wore it that night over a plain white t-shirt with matching *Diadora* trousers, which had pockets half way down the legs. My *Nike* trainers were beaten and old and rubbed my socks thin as I walked. The kids at school would have called them pasties. I thought I looked good. Cute even.

I'd charged up my mp3 player when I got home from school and marched hard to the *Buffy the Vampire Slayer* soundtrack. The graffitied walls and fences gave way to hedges and finally to moss covered walls of the older houses that weren't made of orange bricks.

I was to turn right at the 'Welcome to Maghull' sign, which advised all to drive carefully. I'd have to go past the council houses, round the back of Ashworth Hospital, onto the country roads at the back of the town. This was the fifth time we'd met, and I smiled the whole way. We'd not met in the daytime yet.

Before I met up with him, I always knocked on for Vicky. Her estate was greener than ours. Lawns separated blocks of houses, littered with crisp packets and cans of *Coke*. The houses were made from brown brick and dark wood, which made them look nice from the outside. Her windows were filthy, something my mum would never allow to happen at ours.

'Scrub your windows and wash your nets.' She'd sing to a tune only she knew. 'Hoover your carpets and change your beds.'

Vicky pulled open the door with a stained blue and white chequered tea towel over her left shoulder and her chubby baby brother on her right hip. She wore faded black bottoms from an old *Bon Bleu* tracksuit which were spotted white and pink from bleach, with a green strappy vest. Half-circles had settled under her eyes in the first year, and they'd not disappeared since.

'Oh hiya.' She stepped out. Closed the door slightly behind her, just enough so the lock didn't catch.

'Wanna walk down the farm with me?'

'I can't tonight, mate.' She rolled her eyes toward the baby who stared at me with bright pink cheeks and eyes the colour of pennies found at the bottom of Nan's purse. 'Me mum's out.'

'Shall I text you after?'

She nodded. 'Be careful won't you?'

I snorted. 'Well I'm not gonna…'

She laughed. 'Piss off, that's not what I meant. Just look after yourself. Text me when you're there.'

'Do I look alright?'

'You look lovely.' She didn't look me up and down at all. 'I'm sorry, I've got the tea on. I'll have to get in.'

I half-hugged her so I didn't touch the baby and heard the door close as soon as I'd turned my back.

I made it to the country roads quickly from Vicky's and waited near the farm. Horses moved beyond the wooden fence, black bulking shadow puppets against a purple night sky. Witnessing.

John walked under the yellow lamp lights further up the road. He had this hunched walk. Stiff. Like he expected someone to jump out on him. I walked faster and we met in the twilight between two lampposts.

'Okay?' He had bright blue eyes. I couldn't see them here, just a strip of yellow shine as he looked over my face. He took hold of my hands. 'You're freezing, Ste. Where's your gloves?'

'I don't need gloves.' That was a lie. I'd asked for some on my birthday two weeks ago, but they never got bought. Gloves were the last things my family worried about buying me.

He sighed. 'Wait by Windemere.' He turned and walked back on himself.

I crossed the road to an estate of posh houses. The grass in their gardens had no dandelions or weeds, and they were all cut to exactly the same length. The hedges were trimmed to perfect oblongs with rounded edges and there was no chewy on the paths. I knew he lived in there somewhere, in the rows of warm houses with big TVs, Marksies food, and lovely clothes. I wondered what he'd had for dinner: caviar and vegetables and fresh fruit for dessert. Definitely not a *Fray Bentos*.

I waited at the sign that curved around the mouth of Windermere Road, heard loud voices coming closer. Some of the older kids from school came out of Windermere, laughing like hyenas hunting for some carcass abandoned and left to rot. I lowered my head, turned my body slightly. Rob had already seen me. He was in my year, always out with the older kids.

'What are you doin' round 'ere, ya little faggot?' I'd never noticed before, but he had John's eyes and mouth. His skin was pocked with acne scars, though.

'Come 'ed, lad, the game's gonna start,' one of his mates said.

'I hate him though, lad,' Rob said. 'There's somethin' about him I just can't stand.'

I stared.

'Come 'ed just leave it.'

They left. Rob looked back, but I could breathe again as all of my muscles untangled. My feet and fingers were freezing. I pulled my hands in through the sleeves and rested them across my stomach.

John stood across the street near the entrance to the farm. Had he seen the whole thing with his brother? My face burned red as I crossed over.

'Here.' He slipped gloves over my hands. They were massive; like the scarves Nan used to start knitting and forget to stop, wound round my neck loosely. 'Come on.'

It wasn't late, around six maybe, yet the streets were quiet. In the trees the hoot-hoot of an owl. We turned off the main street and onto the country lane that led up to a single house, veered left to cross a bridge, and wound through the countryside. I didn't know the name of the road, who lived in that house, or what the bridge was called. I called it John's Bridge after him.

My phone vibrated hard in my pocket. I fished it out, held it in both hands, stared into the shining green screen. In grey-black lettering a text from Vicky: 'U OK?'

I pressed button 4 three times, 0 for space, 2 once, 6 once, 0 once, 3 three times, 4 three times, 6 twice, 3 twice.

'Your mum?'

'Vicky. Just checking up.'

'She should just ring. I hate texting.' He grimaced. 'It'll never catch on. Takes too long.'

'Yeah, you're right.' I slipped the phone back into my pocket.

With the shush of some stream or river beneath us and convinced nobody would come by, he put his hand on the back of my head and kissed me. His other hand reached down for my bum and he pulled me closer. Not aggressively, but slowly. Softly. I wrapped my arms around his waist and found it spongy. Cushioned. I liked it. He was bigger than me, wider, taller, smarter, and my trousers got tighter. He wouldn't be able to see.

His tongue was soft and tasted like Listerine. Under that, the faint persistence of a cigarette. I didn't know he smoked. I liked him more. Drew him closer. The soft strums of The Sundays' cover of *Wild Horses* reverberated in my mind. The part in season three where Buffy has her 'perfect high school moment' at the Prom. If we had a Prom would he take me? I'd wear something nice, but he'd look stunning in a black tuxedo and bow tie, his hair slicked back with copious amounts of blue sticky gel from a clear tub with a white label.

When we finally came up for air and sat on the cold concrete, he folded me into his coat to keep me warm.

He kissed my ear and I was beaming. I had butterflies in my chest that swooped like hungry bats. This must be what Buffy felt like when Angel held her. She wanted to be a normal girl as much as I wanted to be a normal boy. But I felt, like she did, maybe that was impossible in the worlds we lived in.

'I'm not using you,' he said.

'I know.' I said it without thinking. I didn't need to think, was unable to, in those hours we spent together.

We held hands as we walked down the lane where nobody ever drove until we reached the main street, crossed over to the park. Parks at night time are eerie things. Like graveyards. Swings lifted and squeaked and even the roundabout turned like the wind was ghost children.

He stung his hand on some tall nettles which grew at the entrance. He hissed as he drew his hand closer to see. We sat on the swings straddle-style so we could face each other. They were wet with rain and I blew on his hand.

'You know, I nearly lost this hand,' he said.

I laughed. 'It's just a sting.'

'No, I mean really.' His eyes locked on mine. 'I had a tumour.'

This was the moment where Buffy would say something sweet and say it softly, describe his hand as perfect then kiss it. Even touch it to her face. I turned away. My face burned despite the cold.

'What happened?' I asked, finally.

'It was taken out,' he said. 'I've got this massive scar across my shoulder. Hate it. Felt like everyone would stare at me in school. Just used to come home and lose myself in books.'

'That sounds lonely.'

'I got used to it.'

That hung in the air between us, a sharp piece of ice on the bitter wind. I knew it needed to be thawed, but I didn't know how.

The wind got stronger, the night colder, and he said, 'You should get going. Bit of a walk back to yours.'

'Yeah,' I said. 'I was just going to say that.' I wasn't. I never would. We kissed one last time at the corner before we turned out of the pitch park onto the lit road. He walked up his street with a spark and puff of smoke. With *Temptation Waits* by Garbage on repeat, I analysed everything we'd done and said. Which wasn't much.

I'm not using you he'd said.

The next morning the school corridors were icy. The single-pane windows clattered like someone just come in from the cold. The old blue laminate tiles were ripped in parts and in others massive blisters had formed filled with air. My feet were heavy from the trek last night and my legs ached.

The music stopped dead in the middle of the Buffy/Angel love suite, *Close Your Eyes* just as each instrument clawed out a crescendo. The mp3 player's screen flashed blue and faded to a bleak grey. Gutted.

The old building, the Molyneux was so quiet at this time of the day. As always, I was in before anyone else arrived. Not even Vicky got into school that early. From the quadrangle, filled with plants, trees, and animals, the gentle rolling trill of wood pigeons.

Footsteps ahead. Someone with squeaky shoes. It was John and he rounded the corner near the library doors. The notices and announcements loosely sellotaped to the frosted windows fluttered as he passed. His blazer fitted perfectly over a green *Adidas* hoody. He looked bulky. Muscular. He scanned the corridor and me and chanced a smile. Nobody was around after all.

His pace quickened. The walk-sprint of he in a desperate hurry. In his hand was a square slip of paper scored with faint blue lines like veins. He passed and the paper was in my eager sweaty hands and it felt hot. A potato baked on one-hundred and twenty degrees, whose skin I couldn't wait to crack and butter.

I tried the library doors, on which a notice for a missing green budgie belonging to Mr Brown of 47 Deyes Lane was stuck to. Mrs Jones mustn't be in the library yet. The door to the cooking room was open and inside smelled like flour and sugar. I dragged a stool close to a work bench. There were names and dates and love hearts from relationships that had died before the end of the year scratched into the worktops with sharp pencils and compasses. I thought about our initials – mine and his – how they'd look in the faded varnish. They'd be too obvious.

I unfolded the creased paper and it smelled like his aftershave. I remembered it from that shop in St John's Precinct. CK One by Calvin Klein. It smelled clean, fresh, edible – like fruit salads in summer.

This was the first time I'd seen his handwriting, and it looked like my little sister's. Massive looping lines and circles over each i and j instead of dots. I felt a pang of embarrassment for him, then for myself as I remembered last night. I know he might have struggled to write it, found it hard to grip the pen and form these words. But he'd taken the time to do it. Maybe every full stop was a jab to his shoulder. Every time he wrote 'and' would feel like the blade of the scalpel bursting open his skin. He'd suffered in writing it but here it was.

He rambled a bit about how his mum had smelled smoke on him when he got home, asked where his gloves were. Before saying he'd written the note so I could throw it away, he moved on in more careful handwriting. Tighter. Smaller, somehow. He'd enjoyed seeing me last night, was sorry if what he'd said had made me feel weird.

'It didn't,' I said to no one.

He wanted to see me that night if I could. I should send him a text message which, as always, would be blank save for a full stop. I imagined him opening his phone to read it. My number wouldn't be saved in the phone's memory and the digits of my number would be grey lines on top of the small green screen.

I sent the full stop straight away.

First class was German. I walked into class just as the scallies were turning the desks around to face the opposite way so when Mr

Vandervelde came in he would be furious.

'Oh 'ere she is, lads,' Rob said. 'Watch your dicks, Sausage is about.'

I didn't look at them, tried to ignore their laughing, and sat down near the front of the class, next to the window.

It was mildly funny to see Vandervelde burst in, arms flailing, spit sputtering from his lips. Furious about the desks. Laughing hysterically, Rob sat at the back, arms sprawled across an entire desk like an ape. Like his friends.

''ey sir, what's German for 'Sausage'.

'Stop this!' Vandervelde shouted.

One of the others flicked through their textbook. '*Wurst*, lad.'

'*Ich liebe Wurst.*' Rob laughed. That high pitched thing, like a train pulling into Lime Street.

My fingers curled into balls, nails dug into the palms of my hands. The shape of Buffy was coming through my skin. '*Dein Bruder liebt Wurst.*'

Vandervelde's mouth fell open.

'What did you say, you queer?' Rob stood up.

'I said your brother's gay.'

He slammed his chest and spread his arms wide. 'You wanna stand up and say that again, lad?'

'It won't make a difference if I stand up or sit down.'

'He's got a bird, you soft little wan-'

'Get out! Get out!' Vandervelde huddled Rob out of the room.

My palms were sweaty, my chest clenched hard and I could hardly breathe. I sat there when class ended, stared out of the window at the sunny day. My breath formed imperfect foggy circles on the glass widening and dissipating with each exhalation.

Two magpies hopped about the glass outside, squawked and rattled and tossed the lifeless, messy carcass of Mr Brown's budgie between each other.

I ate my beans on toast quickly, felt it swish in my stomach as I jogged to make up the twenty minutes lost while my brother was in the bath. I played a CD I'd burned from disc to my computer, Sarah McLachlan's *Surfacing* album. I played *Full of Grace* on repeat from the episode where Buffy had to kill Angel to save the world.

There were no clouds. The odd star shone behind the glare of lanky lampposts. I made my way down through the estate, along the country lane, onto the corner where the path to John's Bridge met the main street. There was nobody here.

Eventually the clouds shrouded the sky, covered the constellations. I was getting colder just stood there. I lifted my feet in succession and rubbed my hands together. My bones were beginning to feel the cold now, too. It was eight o'clock and there I stood.

I text him another full stop and waited. And waited. I took off his massive gloves and left them on the corner to our path about quarter past eight and headed around to Vicky's.

'What's wrong?' She pulled me inside straight away. Her house smelled like stewed meat, but not nice. Like it hung in the air from days ago. 'What's he done to you?'

I couldn't speak. I tried but between sobs it made no sense.

Vicky rang a taxi for me, took a fiver from an empty bottle of whiskey she kept next to the bulb-lit fire inside a fake marble surround. My mum had the same one.

'I'll walk.' I stood up, felt the bare bones of the couch under my hand as I rose and walked the floor.

I made the journey home about nine. Listened to *It Doesn't Matter* by Alison Krauss & Union Station and thought my tears would freeze in the cold. It was six miles home. I walked there.

Judges' Profiles

Kate Johnson (Chair)

Kate is a literary agent at the New York-based Mackenzie Wolf literary agency, representing a range of fiction and nonfiction writers, including short story writers Sam Allingham, Tania Hershman, Bryan Hurt, Bonnie Nadzam, Hasanthika Sirisena and Chloe Wilson. She also adores the stories of Aleksandar Hemon, Lorrie Moore, Eley Williams, Jamie Quatro, Etgar Keret, Mavis Gallant, Shirley Jackson, Joy Williams, and...could really go on and on and on!

Lucy Cowie

Lucy is a freelance editor with over a decade's experience working with a broad range of fiction and non-fiction writers. She started her publishing career at the literary agency LAW and Penguin Random House, before heading to the West Country where she continues to edit for publishers as well as independent writers.

Polly Ho-Yen

Polly is the author of three novels for children, which have been nominated for numerous awards including the Carnegie Medal, Waterstones Children's Book Prize and the Blue Peter Book Award. She worked in publishing for several years and has also been a teacher and recently worked as Reader Development Librarian for Bristol Libraries.

Billy Kahora

Billy's short stories have been published in *Chimurenga, McSweeney's,* Granta Online, *Internazionale, Vanity Fair* and *Kwani.* He was shortlisted for the Caine Prize for African Literature in 2012 and 2014. He wrote the screenplay for the film Soul Boy and co-wrote Nairobi Half Life which both won the Kalasha awards. He has also been editor of the *Kwani Journal* and has run writing workshops for a decade. His short story collection, *The Cape Cod Bicycle War* and other stories was published in 2019. He is lecturer in Creative and Professional Writing at Bristol University.

Acknowledgements

The generous and committed support and contributions of the following people have enabled us to produce a fantastic anthology. A massive thank you to:

The judging panel – Lucy Cowie, Polly Ho-Yen, Kate Johnson and Billy Kahora. Our readers – Georgia Bate, Diane Becker, Jo Borek, Jo Darque, Lu Hersey, Sandra Hopkins, Jeanette Jarvie, Richard Jones, Mike Manson, Bertel Martin, Catherine Mason, Dawn Pomroy, Tom Robinson, Pam Smallwood. Chris Hill, Jonathan Ward, Naomi Clarke and the 3rd year Illustration students at University of the West of England. Tangent Books; Bristol Libraries; Foyles; Peter Morgan and Mark Furneval at ScreenBeetle; Bristol 24/7; And Joe Burt, Nicky Coates, Beccy Golding, Andy Hamilton, Rosa Lovegood, Louis Melia, Natasha Melia, Dave Oakley, Eleanor Pender, Lisa Price, and Thomas Rasche.

And most important of all, enormous thanks to all the writers who had the courage to enter the 2019 Bristol Short Story Prize. It has been the greatest pleasure to read, debate and take inspiration from so many wonderful stories.

2019
Bristol Short Story
Prize Longlist

(a-z by writer's name)

Sarah Frances Armstrong	*All Creatures Great and Small*
Alison Bacon	*Within These Walls*
S. Bhattacharya-Woodward	*Zolo*
Samir Bhimji	*Grace the Worm*
Rua Breathnach	*The Bridge*
Mattie Brennan	*The Last of the Inglorious Revolutionaries*
Sabah Carrim	*The Evil in Me*
Mona Dash	*The Sense of Skin*
Jason Deelchand	*All for Love*
Khadija Dyer	*Salt*
Flic Everett	*The End of the Neighbourhood*
Louise Farr	*Eight Foot Jesus*
Hannah Fox	*Burying Kim*
Marie-Gabrielle Gallard	*black cross*
Lucy Grace	*Sand Seven*
Kavita A. Jindal	*Tulip Persimmon's Head-Wetting*
Rebecca F. John	*The Sea Thief*

Mubanga Kalimamukwento	*The Devil's Ivy*
Sonal Kohli	*The Outing*
Mel Konner	*By the Sea*
Richard Lakin	*Cabbage Trace*
Ferdia Lennon	*Even the Gods*
Rose McDonagh	*Dog's Bone*
Foday Mannah	*Amie Samba*
Michael Morrel	*Interaction*
Rupert Murray	*The Agency on Wilshire Blvd*
Thiva Narayanan	*Sleeper/The Mole*
Sal Page	*I'm Walking*
Nicholas Petty	*These Violent Hands*
Victoria Richards	*The Girl in the Photograph*
Cherise Saywell	*Fellow Travellers*
Claire Snook	*Sarah Turns Sixteen*
Cameron Stewart	*Black Snow*
Carina Swantee	*The Farmhand*
Jo Tiddy	*The Hunter*
Sophie Tiefenbacher	*Tiger Meat*
Liz Tresidder	*from the forest*
Sean Watkin	*I Walked There*
Alison White	*The Butcher's Van*
Colette Willis	*It's So Pretty Here When the Sun Shines*

Winner of the 2019 Sansom Award for Bristol writers:
Alison Bacon *Within These Walls*

Notable Contenders
These stories were in the running for the longlist until the final decisions were made

Ana de Andrada	*Everything is Ready*
Regi Claire	*(Un)certainties*
Louise Finnigan	*Trails*
Rebecca Gabay	*On the Rocks*
Helena Gadelha	*The Brilliance of Dom Pedro II*
Sean Lusk	*A Thick Skin*
Christopher Rowson	*The Butterfly Man*
Martina Ryan	*Kitchen Guy, Husband Guy, Dog*